ALSO BY IAN TREMBLAY

THE ILLEGAL AND THE REFUGEE
An American Love Story
...

AISHA
A Tale of Retribution
...

THE DEATH AND LIFE OF GUSTAV HENN

RICH
HOMELESS
BROKEN
BUT BEAUTIFUL

A NOVEL

IAN TREMBLAY

FOR CECILE

TABLE OF CONTENTS

Chapter 1 - Coming of Age
Page 09

Chapter 2 – Tragedy
Page 65

Chapter 3 - Wanderings
Page 141

Chapter 4 - Coming Home
Page 181

About the Author
Page 219

Chapter 1

COMING OF AGE

Linda Staunton had grown impervious to their advances—impervious, but not indifferent. From boys that is, and later men. Already at a very young age they had begun pursuing her. Chasing her would probably be more exact, and their countless queries were incessant and sometimes laced with an urgency that was certainly more invented than real. It was as if their quests had become their *raison d'être* and their very lives depended on her reaction. Linda had grown accustomed to this multitude of advances; she had learned to deal with them as elegantly and as diplomatically as possible. It was an endless stream of propositions—to go to the movies or to see a show, to just hang out or to go to a football game, to be their girlfriends or to be just friends, and even sometimes, to marry them. In short, to do anything she wanted, now, tomorrow, whenever, whatever. The offers were continuous and incessant and resembled more a bombardment than anything else. The heat had really turned up when she had turned sixteen. Already at that age she was an uncommon beauty, strikingly magnificent, a heart stopper, pure and perfect, strong and stellar, fragile and feminine. She had been gifted with all the best possible physical and mental attributes a human being can posses. When she walked into a room, there was an explosion of brilliance, magnificence, and perfection, comparable to the appearance of a fantastic celestial mega body that renders astronomers and scientists speechless. Her thick black hair was shoulder length, lustrous, and bouncy, curling slightly at the ends, and her eyes were the bluest of blues, as the clear azure of a cloudless summer sky. Her skin was delicate and not too white, more like a cream color with shades of healthy pink. She had an incredibly unique smile. It was inviting and warm and just simply fantastic. It was her best trait, and her grandmother called it "that trillion-dollar smile." Linda was a tall girl who held her head high and carried herself with elegance and grace. She was poised and warm and respectful of all. It was an innate trait of her being and of her character. Life emanated from her with tenderness and passion, and she was inhabited by the fragility and the sensitivity of those beings who, by the very eloquence of their natural persons, are, by definition, beings plus.

In short, Linda Staunton was a stunner, and her life was a constant flow of boys and men coming onto her. She had developed skills to deal with this reality and had learned how to brush them off politely, without hurting their feelings, or how to slide out of a situation, gently but firmly. Guys were so predictable in their approaches, always using the same lame lines, that it made it easy for her. It was as if they were begging to be brushed off. A lot of times they would just come up to her and gawk, or utter some predictable banality, or even yet, be such awkward idiots and totally unable to express the most basic emotion that it was easy for her to send them packing. Of course, with some guys she had to be firmer, because they just did not get the brush off, or they were so full of themselves that they could not believe she was politely saying no. The multiplicity of these situations gave Linda a lot of power and made the other girls intensely jealous; she did not abuse that power, however, and treated every girl with respect and kindness and continuously downplayed the effect she had on her male entourage. Linda Staunton was not pretentious about her beauty. She carried it with grace and dignity; exceptional beauty could not have been given to a kinder or a more generous person. Sometimes life in the distribution of its blessings does things right. This was one of those times.

Once, she had been in an airport lounge waiting to take off to Florida for spring break with three of her girlfriends. They were waiting for their plane to be called when an older gentleman approached them. He was dressed in a very elegant beige suit, with a matching shirt and a large, colorful bowtie. His freshly cut hair was clean, white as snow, and fell to his shoulders. On his head was a large *café au lait* brimmed hat, the kind you see worn by lifelong residents of the Caribbean. He walked with the help of a most unusual black sculptured cane, which could have come from the confines of Africa or some other exotic and mysterious place.

He slowly came up to where Linda and her friends were sitting and with great poise and confidence; he tipped his hat in Linda's direction and said, "Excuse me, miss, although I am sure I am quite out of line here and I do not want in any way to seem rude or anything, but I must confess that I have been observing you for the past twenty minutes or so from over there." He pointed to the other end of the lounge with his cane. "And I just had to come over here to confirm what I saw. I must say my eyesight is better that I thought. You miss, are the most exquisitely beautiful woman I have seen in a very, very long time, and believe me, I know these things." He smiled to Linda, just looking at her for a few seconds, and buried deep in his pale blue eyes was a mischievous twinkling, a *je ne sais quoi* of unforgettable memories and past encounters with love and beauty. Linda blushed and looked at him in shock, unable to speak; she managed a nervous smile and blurted out,

"Well ... eh ... thank you, sir." She turned toward her girlfriends for support, but they just shrugged in unison and said nothing.

"You're very welcome, miss." He smiled to her again, tipped his hat, and said to her girlfriends, "Ladies, please excuse my most impolite intrusion, and I do wish you all a very pleasant trip." He turned and walked gracefully back to where he had come from.

The girls had nervously giggled it off, but Linda had been touched and surprised by the gentleman's approach. At the time she was still young and unsure of herself and when people walked up to her like that, it freaked her out quite a bit; she thought it was just too much. She was conflicted about her looks, and she always had been. She both hated and loved the reaction of men to her looks. She knew it gave her power in a sense, yet she was unsure about what to do with it, if anything at all. It was scary at times, and she could not really talk about these fears or thoughts to anyone, especially not her mother, who considered her looks an asset that would help her get ahead in life. To Linda, it was just the way she looked, and she wished everybody wouldn't make such a big deal about it. She wanted more out of life than just to be pretty, and that was one of the reasons why she studied so hard. Her ambition was to become a veterinarian and to work with animals. She loved animals, and it was a job she knew she would love, but most of all, she wanted to prove to herself and to the world that she could do something useful and meaningful with her life and not just be the prettiest girl on the block.

There was, however, one lesson that life had taught Linda Staunton more than anything else, and that was poverty. She knew about poverty and how it was to be poor—dirt poor that is. She had been raised in it, real poverty—the one that is closer to misery than anything else. Her mother had raised her and her two sisters and one brother single-handedly. Her father had disappeared one day when Linda was nine; she vaguely remembered him. Her mother had been thirty at the time, and her sisters and brother were seven, five, and four. It had been very hard on all of them, especially her mom. She had had no time to brood on the whereabouts of her deadbeat husband, however, and to feed and care for her children became her one and only priority. She had gotten a job at a local factory and Linda's grandmother Florence, or Grandma Flo, as they all affectionately called her, came over five days a week to help with the chores and with the children. How cruelly in those young years Linda had felt the wrath of poverty. There was never enough of anything, and her mother's wages barely covered the rent and the food, never mind the doctors' bills, medicine, clothes, school supplies, and so on. The list was long of things they needed and had to go without. Every penny was accounted for, every slice of bread calculated, leftovers became tomorrow's meals, clothes were passed on down to the young, as were shoes. Linda remembered once how a pair of semi-white shoes that had belonged to her had been passed on down to her younger brother Derek. She had felt so bad for him at the time. It was bad enough for him that they were girl's shoes, but the worst was that the black polish her mother had used to make them black did not hide all the white. At the time, Derek had been devastated, and to him it had seemed like the end of the world.

"It's okay Derek, no one will notice. You know, it doesn't show that much. Just wear your pants real low, okay?" Linda had done her best to uplift his spirits at what he considered to be a catastrophe. His baby blue eyes were filled to the brim, and tears rolled down his round pink cheek.

"I'd rather go barefoot, Linda," he sniffled, wiping the tears from his cheek. "Everybody will laugh at me; I don't want to go to school."

Linda took him by the shoulders and looked him straight in the eyes. "Look, Derek, I promise no one will make fun of you, okay? I will see to that. Just remember to wear your trousers really low, you got that?" Linda gave him her best smile, and he half smiled back, only partially reassured.

"Okay, Linda, thanks," he added while wiping his tears with both his forearms.

Of course the other boys and girls at school made fun of him, with all the cruelty of boys and girls of that age. As a matter of fact, they had a field day with it, for days Derek suffered the constant and vicious rile of his peers. He resisted well to their attacks, all things considered, and had been strong in the face of adversity of the worst kind.

Linda had never forgotten that. God she had felt bad for poor little Derek. It had broken her heart. She knew that what her brother was going through was because of their poverty, their deep, absolute poverty. It was the kind of poverty that leaves wounds, profound wounds, on all those who live and exist in its formidable grip, especially children. For Linda, her brother, her sisters, and her mother, poverty was their shepherd and their keeper; they belonged to poverty, as it belonged to them. It reminded them of that every day, with the occasional pangs of hunger or the unavailability of simple necessities. They lived within the confines of its invisible boundaries, prisoners of their dire economic conditions and burdened with its inherent humiliation. In a country that idealizes wealth and the accumulation of property, they were on the low end of every scale.

Linda had suffered tremendously all through her youth because of her family's condition. When she was little, she had actually believed for a long time that poverty was as present inside a person as it was visible from their exterior. She thought that people who saw them walk down the street could actually see through them and instantly knew they were poor, no matter how carefully her mother had dressed or cleaned them. To have lived up close and personal with poverty at a young age was a bitter lesson that life had imposed on her. Linda had been profoundly hurt and ashamed of her family's condition; it had been the dominating sentiment of her youth

Linda helped her mother as much as she could with the chores and the kids' homework. Her grandparents also did all they could, although they were not rich and subsided on her grandfather's meager pension. They were always there for them, especially her grandmother Flo, and although she suffered terribly from arthritis, she never once complained. She cooked and cleaned and scolded and encouraged, always cheerfully energetic and always strong. She was the rock that they all hung unto in their time of desperate need.

For the Stauntons' there was never any vacation in Florida, or summer trips to Maine, or weekends at Disney World or Las Vegas. No car either, or any other luxury of any kind whatsoever. There was nothing in their lives that was not essential; it was the nature of their condition. They did, however, have the love they had for each other. For Linda this was everything. She loved her family fiercely and they loved her back, equally unconditionally. Love was the bond that united them and kept them close and strong. As for the exterior world, well, Linda had a built an armor to deal with that, and

IAN TREMBLAY

she used it to put on a defiant face when she needed to do so, even though she was burning and suffering inside. There had been so many nights that she had cried herself to sleep, cursing the world for having been born poor, that she had lost count. All the hurt and pain of those early years had thickened the foundation of her heart and soul and had made her a stronger, better person. She did not realize this at the time, and that realization would not come to her until much later in her life and then, that was under very different circumstances.

Then, in her last years at high school, things began to change for Linda Staunton, a change that helped put her family's poverty on the back burner, at least in her mind. Boys began acting differently with her, and they became overly attentive, showering her suddenly with compliments and invitations. It confused her at first; she did not understand what was going on and did not fully realize that over the course of the past few years her features and body had changed dramatically. They had exploded, and she had become a spectacularly beautiful young girl. Everyone in her presence, whether male or female, was awed by her looks, and it took her a while to adjust to that. It did help, however, to make those last years in high school joyous ones for her, even though the situation at home remained the same. She was the undeclared star of the school, and just about every boy was secretly or openly attracted or infatuated with her and wanted to date her. Of course, this situation made a lot of the girls bitterly jealous, especially Diane Sorenson. Diane considered Linda a nobody, someone who had nothing to offer—no family connections, no money, no parties, no clothes, or car. In short, she was nothing and had to be totally ignored. That was exactly what Diane Sorenson and her coterie of fans and hangers on had always done. After all, there was nothing in the world that Linda

Staunton had that they wanted—well, except for her looks maybe and her boyfriend.

"Watch out for that little bitch," Diane would hiss. "She will steal all of our boyfriends. She's poison, be very careful. I mean, shit, she doesn't even have one single decent thing to wear; can you believe that? I don't get it, guys are such morons. It should be illegal for them to make their own choices." Her coterie nodded their heads in approval, as they always did. None of them would ever have dared to challenge her about anything anyway, especially about how she felt about Linda Staunton.

"What does Richard see in her anyway?" Diane was referring to Richard Benson, the very talented quarterback of their high school football team and all-around hunk extraordinaire. Richard Benson was six feet two with blond hair and blue eyes and a zillion gallons of charm. He was the favorite conversation subject of just about every girl in school. He was the catch of the catches; it enraged Diane to the extreme that he had chosen Linda Staunton as a girlfriend. She seethed with envy and jealousy.

"Maybe he's light in the head or something," a steaming Diane led her friends down the school corridor, fueled by her own sense of unfairness and rage. "I think he's been knocked around too much playing football, and well, he certainly has a problem seeing correctly." Her sarcasms about Linda's looks were legion, "oh well, who cares anyway." Her entourage made no comment. After all, Linda's looks were to all of them self-evidently astounding. It was a blatant truth that even Diane's blind jealousy could not change and that they cautiously kept to themselves. Just as they turned a corner, the group saw Linda and Richard hand in hand walking their way. Diane slowed down and began swaying her hips suggestively.

She kept her head high and looked directly at Richard as the group passed the couple.

"Hello, Richard." She looked him straight in the eyes, smiling enticingly and ignoring Linda completely.

"Oh hi, Diane, ladies," Richard smiled to them all as he and Linda passed them by.

"Hi, Richard," all the other girls behind Diane answered together in unison.

Richard turned toward Linda and gave her his, "Hey, what can I say?" smile. Linda smiled back.

"I love you when you smile like that, Richard Benson. You're so bloody loveable," she said and laughed heartily.

"What do you mean?" He shrugged and had an innocent look on his face.

"You know what, don't play dumb now." She looked at him with a touch of mischief.

"Okay, I was just trying to be nice, that's all. I do have to be nice and polite to everybody, you know."

"Yeah, I know you do. Just don't forget that you're mine."

"Linda, I love you and only you. You're my all and everything. I don't care about those other girls." He pointed with his thumb backward to the girls they had just passed.

"Neither do I," she quickly responded. They looked at each other and he realized that she had been pulling his leg a bit, and they both broke out laughing.

Although they were now well past the girls and Diane Sorenson, their complicity and laughter echoed loudly against the cold gray school corridors, pounding Diane Sorenson's oversized ego with their joy and their love. Diane was seething, she put up a solid front for her entourage, but deep inside her conniving heart, the smoldering seeds of intense jealousy, were ignited and burning furiously.

Yes, those were happy times for Linda, and there was no impediment to her happiness, except for Diane Sorenson's intense jealousy maybe, but she didn't let that get to her too much. All through high school she felt like she was on a cloud; her grades were excellent, she was popular and best of all she and Richard were madly in love. They were completely devoted to each other and filled to the brim of their beings with a love that was pure and unspoiled and intense and unconditional.

Linda had found a part-time job at a fast food outlet, and with the money she earned, she helped her family. It was the happiest time of her young life. Sometimes when she was alone in her bed at night, she would shed a silent tear, not of sorrow, but because she was happy that life was being good to her at last, after all the sufferings she had endured in her younger years.

One night, a few weeks before their graduation, she and Richard were lying in his bed at his parents' house. His parents had gone to a concert, and Richard and Linda were supposed to be studying, but they had decided that making love was a better option. Linda took Richard's head in her hands and brought her face up to his. They were eyeball to eyeball.

"Richard, I want to be yours forever. I don't want to know anyone else, ever; promise me we will always be together and that nothing and no one will ever come between us." Linda's eyes were ablaze with love and passion; her skin still flushed from their lovemaking.

"Oh Linda, I promise. God, I promise. I love you so much it hurts. I will always be yours and yours alone, always, I promise." He touched her lips gently with his own, grazing them with his breath. She responded with her tongue, taking his mouth into hers, and their bodies were instantly ignited again with the fury of their youth.

Later, as they lay in the warmth and afterglow of their release, Linda turned toward Richard and propped her head up on one of her elbows. She passed her other hand through his hair, and he moaned and opened his eyes.

"Hey, what's up?"

"I really don't like this idea of us being apart, Richard. I mean you at your college and me at my veterinarian school. I understand why we will be in different schools, but I don't have a good feeling about it, and I just wish we could stay together. I can't live far away from you like that, and it hurts me just to think about it." Richard took her free hand and began to kiss it lightly.

"I know, sweetheart, but, we've talked about this before. It's the best place for me to play football and there are no other options, you know that. Plus, we'll only be a three-hour drive apart. I'll be up there to see you every weekend, I promise. You know I can't live without you either. It'll be hard, but it's only for a few years, then we'll be together for the rest of our lives. Promise me that you'll give this an honest try and that you won't worry too much, please."

She looked at him with sadness in her eyes,

"Okay, I promise," she said without much conviction and cuddled up to him, laying her head on his chest. He put his arm around her and kissed the back of her head.

"It's just that I have a bad feeling about this. I can't really explain it. We won't be together, and I hate that idea, that's all." She held onto him tightly.

Richard stroked her hair gently and continued to kiss her head.

"I'll be with you. I'll always be with you. I'll never leave you, I swear, never. Just remember, even when we're apart, we're together," he whispered in her ear. She did not respond but stayed glued to his body and soon fell fast asleep.

An hour later, Richard nudged her,

"Linda, wake up, my parents will be home soon."

They got up and got dressed in silence and then headed downstairs to where they had left their homework.

That night, after Richard brought her home, Linda lay awake in her bed, eyes wide open.

"Why does love have to be so good and so scary?" she pondered. "Why am I afraid? What am I afraid of?" The answers to her questions never came that night, and after a few hours of useless soul searching and staring at the ceiling, slumber finally came and released her from her teenage existential queries.

Graduation came and went, and the summer flew by. It was a wonderful summer, filled with the sanctity of their love and the promise of a bright future. They were bubbly and excited about their imminent departures for school and the perspective of meeting new people and discovering new places. They made plans and dreamed about the future, their future, the one in which they would be together forever.

The end of summer came too quickly for the young lovers. The time to say good-bye had arrived and they would each have to go their separate ways. They had been together every single day for the past three years, and an unsettling sentiment filled the air. Richard would be the first to leave. His parents would drive him to his school, and Linda would leave later that afternoon by bus. She walked over to his house in the morning to see him off. They had agreed to no tears, no sadness, just a, "Good luck, my love, and see you in two weeks"—easier said than done, of course.

Richard's mother opened the door.

"Oh, hi, Linda, come on in please. We're just about ready to go."

"Hi, Mrs. Benson, how are you?"

"A bit sad, but excited also. I do hope he makes it to the big leagues." The last part she whispered. She wasn't supposed to say that; it spooked Richard out. Linda nodded her head, her eyes opened wide in approval as she let herself in.

Richard and his father came down the stairs loaded with luggage.

"Hi, Richard, Mr. Benson, all ready to go, eh?" Linda said as cheerfully as she could, while flashing her bravest smile.

"Yeah, I think so. Anyway, if I forget anything, my parents will certainly take care of it," Richard said ironically while making a face in the direction of his overprotective mother. His mother smiled, oblivious to his comment.

"Okay, people, let's get this stuff in the car and get going." Richard's father moved toward the door with Richard in tow.

"I'll go get my purse and be right there." Mrs. Benson's voice was a bit high pitched, revealing how tense she was. Richard was her only child, and this was a big thing for her.

Once the car was loaded and Richard's parents were sitting in it, the lovers stood facing each other in a tender embrace.

"I'll call you later, okay?"

"You'd better not forget, or in two weeks I'll poke your eyes out, Richard Benson." Linda kept a brave face; she had learned that when she was young. Her heart, however, was heavy and laden with sorrow.

"I love you," she whispered in his ear.

"I love you too," he whispered in hers. His father honked the car horn,

"Come on, let's go, Richard," he shouted.

Richard let her go and got into the car. He closed the door, his eyes never leaving hers as they drove away. Once they were at a distance, tears began to pour down Linda's face. Richard was far now, and he couldn't see that she was crying. The accumulated anguish and apprehension of the last few days came pouring out of her, and for a long time she stood there on the curb, immobile, unable to tear herself away, her body shaking from her profound and sincere despair. After a very long time, she turned and walked slowly away, head down, shoulders drooping, completely dejected and depressed.

At about the same time on the other side of town, in the pompously named gated community called Alcove of Paradise, where people of substantial means lived, Diane Sorenson was getting into her parents' luxury car for the drive to college. Diane smiled, content; she was off to the same college as Richard Benson, and the thought that Linda Staunton would not be around to interfere in her plans pleased her immensely. She had decided that she would have Richard Benson, and that she would do whatever was necessary to make that happen, no matter what it was, and by whatever means.

"Linda Staunton, you're history, you little trashy bitch. I'll show you how the game is played," she said to herself and smiled as she let herself slip down into the comfortable leather seat of the car. She closed her eyes, comforted by the thought that she now had the advantage. "What a mistake you've just made," she surmised, "to let Richard Benson go off alone to the same college as me! Talk about stupid. Now this is where having money makes a difference," she concluded. But then again, as Diane well knew, Linda had had no choice. Her financial situation did not permit her to go to this college or any other college and it was only because of her excellent grades that Linda would be off to the state veterinarian school. Diane Sorenson was convinced that all this was destiny and that destiny was, absolutely and rightly so, on her side.

Linda left for school later that afternoon. She took a cab with her mother to the bus station, and they hugged and said their good-byes. Her mother's eyes swelled up with tears. Linda was her eldest, and she had never been away for any extended period of time.

"Oh, come on, Mom, I'll be okay. I swear, it's a safe town, plus I'm living on campus in a girl's residence that has 24/7 security, so what in the world can happen? Nothing, so please stop worrying about me. I'll be okay, I promise." Her mother wiped her tears with her hands and looked Linda straight in the eyes.

"I know sweetheart, I know. Someday when you're a mother you'll understand how I feel. I know you'll be okay." They hugged again, and her mother held onto Linda tightly.

"Mom, will you be okay with the children and work and all? I worry about that. I mean, Granny Flo's health is not that good anymore and ..."

"Hush, hush now, you just go and get yourself an education, be the best of your class, and leave the worrying to me"

"I'll work very hard, Mom, I promise."

"I know you will." They looked at each other one last time and smiled. Linda detached herself from her mother's embrace, kissed her on the forehead, and boarded the bus. Her mother watched the bus pull away with a mix of apprehension and hope. Slowly, she made her way back to the waiting taxi.

It was a six-hour bus ride to her destination, but it went by really fast. Linda was excited. A new school, new people, new everything—she couldn't wait. She only wished Richard was with her. He was so strong and so solid, she always felt safe with him, and there were never any questions or apprehensions.

Soon enough, she was in her room at the Arlene Robinson Residence for Women. Mrs. Robinson apparently had been a very generous contributor to the school, enough so that they had named the building after her. The room was small, but it had a nice cozy feeling to it and from her window, Linda could see the green and flowered grounds of the school and the warm countryside that surrounded it. Mrs. Wright, who was in charge of the women's residence, had taken care of Linda upon her arrival. She had given her a short history lesson about the place and the surrounding area. Mrs. Wright was a stocky, heavyset woman, with short, neatly arranged hair, and had a very austere and serious look about her.

"This is not a place for pleasure, Miss Staunton; this is a serious school that expects you to behave accordingly and to keep your grades up. Now, do you understand the rules of the residence? Have I made myself clear enough?"

"Yes, Mrs. Wright, and thank you very much for the explanations and the tour. Everything is very clear, and once again, thank you."

"Very well then, get settled in, and if you have any questions, you know where to find me."

"Yes, of course, thank you." Linda closed the door, and Mrs. Wright walked briskly down the corridor and was probably off to intimidate some other new arrival.

Linda looked about the room; she had never slept anywhere but in her own bed at home. It would be a new and strange feeling for her. She got busy unpacking her things.

About forty-five minutes later, there was a light knock on the door. Linda came out of the bathroom, where she had been busy putting her things into place.

"Yes?" She called out to the door.

Someone opened the door, and the head of a girl of about her age appeared in the doorway. She had a generous crop of red hair, the bluest eyes, and an infectious smile on her freckled face.

"Hi, I'm Peggy, your next door neighbor. I saw you pass by with *Mrs. Uptight Wright.*" Her smile was generous and friendly. Linda walked toward her smiling and with her hand outstretched.

"Hi, I'm Linda, Linda Staunton. Come on in." Peggy opened the door and took Linda's hand.

"No, I'll let you settle in, but we could grab a bite to eat at the cafeteria when you're done. What do you say?"

"I'd love to, Peggy; just give me another fifteen minutes or so."

"Okay, great. I'll come back to get you. See you then." She left, closing the door as she went.

Later she and Peggy shared a pizza and some sodas. It was as if they had been friends forever. They talked for hours about their families, their friends, their boyfriends, and their dreams. Peggy was from a large city, and she was quick and streetwise, which was new and fascinating for Linda. Linda felt lucky to have already made such a great friend. She was excited about the school and Peggy and about her new surroundings, but she missed Richard a lot that first day, "Oh Richard, I wish you were here with me now, in my arms and kissing me."

Meanwhile, Richard's arrival at college had been quite different. His college was one of the top schools in the country. Everything, be it the buildings, the grounds, the curriculum, or the professors, was first class. Richard and his parents had been really impressed by how they had taken care of him on arrival. Of course, Richard's football talents were well known here. The college had gone to considerable trouble to have him enroll there and play football for the team. They had accepted him even though his grades were below the required level for admission. Richard had promised he would work hard to make his grades better, and the college had accepted that pledge with the help of a lot of coaxing from the team's football coach. Richard had his own fully furnished apartment off campus. The football team paid for all his expenses. He even had the use of a small car, which, although it was the property of the school, was reserved for his exclusive use. The football coach, Mr. Warren, had taken Richard and his parents on a tour of the school and then had invited them to lunch at one of the better restaurants in town.

"Mr. and Mrs. Benson, you can be assured that Richard will be well treated and taken care of here. We will also see to it that his grades are kept up and that he stays out of trouble." He smiled and winked to Richard in a gesture of complicity. "You know how young people are, but trust me, we are well organized here, and we apply very strict rules for school, recreation, and of course, football." He turned toward Richard. "We have great faith in you, young man, and we are showing you that faith today. I do hope you will not let us or your parents down." He eyeballed Richard with intensity, his whole demeanor laden with authority.

Richard cleared his throat. "Thank you very much, Mr. Warren, for putting your faith in me, and believe me, I won't let you or my parents down, sir, and that's a promise."

"That's the spirit, young man. That's what we want to hear from you." Richard turned toward his mother and smiled at her. His mother smiled back, beaming with motherly pride and joy. She could hardly believe that her Richard, her only child, was now off into the world and on his own. Her eyes became misty, and she squeezed her husband's hand hard.

Richard's thoughts drifted toward Linda, his sweet, adorable Linda. "I wonder how she's making out alone. I hope she's okay," he pondered. "God, I miss her, I can't wait to call her tonight." When he thought about her, he went off into another place, a place that was warm and comforting and that belonged only to them. His father's question brought him back from his thoughts.

"Don't you agree with Mr. Warren, Richard?" Richard had no idea what they were talking about. It was like that when he thought about Linda—his mind drifted off, and it was as if she had entered his body, and he would became oblivious to everything and to all.

"Yes, of course, Dad, Mr. Warren, of course, totally," he jumped in and smiled. They were content, unaware of the fact that he had missed the last part of the conversation. Mr. Warren paid the bill even though Richard's father protested.

"Mr. and Mrs. Benson, today you are the guests of the school. Thank you very much for coming, and I do hope we will see you again soon." Mr. Warren was a large, likable man whose smile inspired confidence and trust. Across the table the Bensons held each other by the hand and beamed with complete parental joy and admiration.

After they left the restaurant, Richard and Mr. Warren saw his parents off. His mother got very emotional, and Richard put his arms around her. He was a full-grown man now, and his broad, athletic shoulders engulfed her completely.

"Hey, come on, Mom, I'm a big boy now. I don't want you to worry about me, okay, promise?" His mother broke from his embrace and wiped a tear from her cheek. She looked up to Richard and smiled.

"Yes, okay, I promise, but call me often, will you?" Her voice was cracking, and her eyes were filled with all the emotions provoked by the now-empty nest that awaited her back home, emotions that had been building up for months and that were now rising to the surface.

"Of course, Mom, I'll call you often, I promise." Richard kissed his mother and shook his father's hand.

"You work hard and listen to Mr. Warren now, son." His father shook Mr. Warren's hand, thanking him profusely for everything.

"Thanks Dad, Mom," Richard was all smiles as he waved them off in the departing car.

"Fine people, your parents Richard. Okay, son, you had better go and get settled in now. School starts soon, and so does football practice. So go on now, scoot and get a head start on things."

"Yes sir, Mr. Warren, and thanks again for everything."

"Think nothing of it, son. Hey, do you need help to find that apartment again? I could show you …"

"It's okay, sir," Richard interrupted. "I know exactly where it is. I have an excellent memory." He tapped a finger on his temple. "I'll be fine. Thanks for everything again, sir. It was very nice of you, and I appreciate it. I'll see you at your office tomorrow at ten a.m."

"Okay, Richard, it's been my pleasure. I'll see you tomorrow then. Oh, and by the way, you'll get to meet some of the other players tomorrow; we've got a great bunch of guys, you'll see."

"I look forward to it, sir." Richard shook his hand and began to walk away. "Bye now."

"Yeah, good-bye, Richard."

Richard stopped for some groceries and then headed to the apartment. He unpacked his things quickly and then sat comfortably in front of the television to watch a game. He put his feet up on a low table and sunk into the couch with a cold beer in his hands. "Life is sweet," he surmised. "God, life is sweet." After the game he sent Linda a text saying he loved her and that everything had gone really well. She texted back that she loved him too and missed him and would have a lot to tell him that evening. They had agreed to text as often as they liked but to try to talk on the phone every day if possible.

"Baby, baby, I miss you," Richard shouted, moving about the apartment holding the phone to his ear, his other arm gesticulating wildly in all directions; he had had a few beers, and he was excited and happy and wanted to share his joy with Linda.

"Oh me too, Richard, me too, I miss you so much. I wish you were here with me," she shrieked, twisting and turning in every direction of the main lobby of the residence. She was excited and her voice was a notch higher than usual. A security guard, a heavyset black woman sitting at a desk near the front door of the residency, sent her a disapproving look. Linda lowered her voice, "I can't wait to be in your arms again and to touch you and kiss you. Oh, Richard, I miss you so much." Richard moaned and sent her several loud smooches.

"I kiss every square inch of that incredible body of yours, my love and especially those wonderful lips."

Linda broke out laughing. "Oh, Richard, you're so bad," she squealed. "Hey, you know what, Richard? The school is really great, and I love it, plus, everyone has been super nice, and you know what else? I've made a new friend. Her name is Peggy. I can't wait for you to meet her. She's really cool and sweet, and it's like we've known each other forever. Can you believe that?"

"Oh really, baby, wow, that's great. I'm so happy for you." The lovers' conversation continued on, bubbly and oblivious to everything and to all, their chatter punctuated with multiple and repeated declarations of love, kissing noises and squeals of excitement. For over one hour they explained to each other in minute detail their new surroundings and the people in it. It was as if they had not spoken for months when in fact it had only been a few hours.

"In fourteen days I'll be up to see you, I can't wait," Richard whispered languorously.

"Me neither, baby. It's unbearable. It's going to be a long fourteen days," Linda said and giggled nervously. Finally the two young lovers hung up, each with his or her heart heavy, unable, because of the distance that separated them, to consume the desire that burned their bodies or to cure the ache that filled their hearts and souls.

When Richard showed up two weekends later, the young lovers were fused together. They stayed in the bed of their rented motel room most of the time and made love continuously. They even ordered food in and ate in bed. It was the first time they had ever been separated for such a long period of time, and they just could not get enough of each other. The explosion of their pent-up love was like the eruption of a long silent volcano, whose power and potency had been contained for long time and who could at last rain mountains of fire and rocks on its surroundings and rumble thunderously, shaking the earth with the vibrations of its complete contentment.

Alas, it was all over too quickly. Richard had to head back, and the parting was hard on both of them. Back at the residency, Linda sat in her room alone, depressed. The door opened slightly.

"Anybody home?" Peggy called out.

"Yeah, I'm here." Linda replied sullenly.

Peggy walked in.

"Oh, are we a bit sad?" Peggy asked, as if talking to a baby. She sat on the bed beside Linda, lowering her head trying to make eye contact with her; Linda was staring at the floor. "Come on, now, let's go have a coffee and talk girl talk. What do you say?" Linda turned slightly toward her and managed a smile.

"Okay, Peggy, anything but sitting here alone and thinking about Richard. I miss him so much it hurts." Tears began to roll down her cheeks, and Peggy took her in her arms and hugged her.

"Oh, it'll be okay. You'll see him again soon. Come on now, let's go." She took Linda's hand and got her to get up, and Linda wiped the tears from her face.

"Thanks, Peggy. I'm such a baby. It's just that when I'm not with Richard, it hurts me here." Linda passed her hand on her stomach to indicate where it hurt. "Do you think I'm normal?" Peggy smiled.

"Yeah, you're normal. I've been there. I know the feeling. Don't worry, everything will be all right. Think about the next time you'll see him. Won't that be something now? It's not that far off, you know."

"Yeah, I know. I'm sorry, Peggy, I'm so immature. Okay, let's go." They headed toward the residency cafeteria; Linda put her arm around Peggy's waist as they walked down the corridor.

"Thanks, Peggy. Thanks for being my friend and understanding me." Linda looked toward her.

"Oh, stop it now. That's what friends are for, right?" Peggy looked at her and smiled.

"Yeah, that's what friends are for." Linda put her head on Peggy's shoulder, and a smile had come back on her face.

Meanwhile, Diane Sorenson had been busily at work. Her plan to have Richard Benson was taking shape. She had done her homework, and a little flirting with a clerk at the admissions office had provided Richard's address, phone number, and school schedule. Plus, she had gotten a schedule of the football team's games and practices from the sports department, and as she was in two of Richard's classes, she organized things so as to have a few accidental encounters with him.

One bright and sunny Tuesday morning, two weeks after classes had started; Richard was walking briskly to his first class of the day.

"Richard, Richard Benson, wait up." It was Diane who was coming up behind him. She wore a short red summer skirt made of a very light and fluid fabric. Her semi-transparent white blouse was transparent just enough so that one could see the outline of her firm breasts sitting in a pretty pink bra. She wore an expensive pair of red sandals, and her toenails were painted a matching color. She had spent hours that morning doing her hair and makeup in anticipation of her encounter with Richard. On one of her shoulders and to one side, hung by only one strap, was a small black leather backpack. The pressure of the one strap on her blouse opened it just enough for some cleavage to show. In her loose hand she carried a few books. Of course the look and the encounter were all part of her meticulous plan. Richard had turned and waited for her to catch up.

"Hi, Richard, can I walk with you to class?" Diane gave him her best smile as she caught up with him.

"Sure, Diane," he gave her a quick look over and couldn't help but notice how sexy she looked. "So, Diane, how have you been?" He asked her as they began to walk together toward class.

"I thought you'd never ask, Richard Benson. We've been here nearly three weeks, and you've barely spoken a word to me. I mean, we are from the same town and the same school, you know?"

"I know, Diane. I'm sorry, but I've been really caught up in football practice and school and also, every second weekend, I go see Linda, and I don't have much time left for anything else." Richard's eyes kept falling toward her cleavage as they walked. Even though his glimpses only lasted a few seconds, Diane took note of the effect she was having on him.

"But still, a little more than just hello would be nice." She gave him a mischievous smile, but she did not overdo it. "Anyway, to answer your question, Richard, I'm fine, thank you for asking. I miss my friends a lot, though. Also, you know James and I split up just before I left for school, and I've been single since then, and to be honest with you, I feel a bit lonely sometimes. Plus, I still haven't made any new friends here. I've been too busy with school and all that, you know." Her tone was meant to induce compassion and even a little pity from Richard, and it worked.

"Oh come on, Diane, you'll make new friends in no time, and a boyfriend won't be a problem. I mean, look at you. You are an amazingly beautiful woman. All these city guys here at college will be hounding you soon, mark my words."

"You're just saying that because I'm a bit down right now, Richard. You've never told me I was beautiful before. Do you really mean that?" Diane looked toward him, her eyes begging for an affirmative answer.

"Diane, I really mean it, okay? You're very beautiful and charming, and I've always thought very highly of you. I think you have great potential. I mean, you're not just beautiful, you are also intelligent and a really sharp person. We just never got to know each other much, because, well, I've been seeing Linda for all these years, and we never had the chance to talk. But there you are; now you know."

"Oh, Richard, thank you, that's very sweet of you. It really makes me feel good. As for me, well I've always had a lot of respect and admiration for you. You are really a person that I look up to. It's funny how we went to the same school for four years and we never had a real conversation. Isn't that weird?"

"Well, better late than never, Diane," they smiled to each other.

"Well maybe we can have a drink or a bite to eat sometime—you know, to make up for lost time and to talk about the hometown. What do you say?" Diane eyed him from the corner of her eye to measure his reaction.

"Sure, why not? I'll tell you what, Diane. Tomorrow after football practice, what do you say we go for some pizza and a few beers? Is that a deal?" Richard's proposition was sincere and a bit naïve and he did not really know what he was getting into. He just wanted to be nice to someone from his hometown who he believed was lonely and homesick.

"I'd love that, Richard. Thank you, that's very kind and generous of you. I really appreciate it."

"It's nothing. Come on, so it's a date for tomorrow then?" He smiled.

"Yeah, it's a date." Diane was beaming; it had been easier than she had thought. Richard was convinced that there was no harm done to have some pizza and a conversation with her. Of course, any self-respecting conniving female could have told him he was being played, but Richard, as most guys, was oblivious to the strategic intricacies of feminine charm tactics.

As they got close to the building they were headed to, Diane pretended to trip and her books flew forward out of her hand. She grabbed Richard by the arm to break her fall and then, quickly ran toward her books and bent forward to retrieve them. She bent without bending her knees, and in such a way that she was sure that Richard would get a good glimpse up her short skirt. Diane had worn a very sexy pink G-string especially for this moment. She took an extra second or two before standing upright again and then turned in his direction and noticed that his face had turned crimson red.

"Thank you for breaking my fall, Richard. I could have fallen and hurt myself," she said in a very innocent little girl voice while arranging her skirt.

A very flustered Richard stuttered, "Are you okay? I mean, did you hurt yourself?"

"No, I'm fine, thanks." She smiled, happy to see him blushing and at a loss for words.

Richard's mind was flooded with thoughts of her ass in the pink G-string, and he was very troubled by his thoughts. Diane's plan had worked to perfection.

They sat side by side in class, and Diane put her glasses on and pretended to be very absorbed in the professor's lecture. She crossed and uncrossed her legs every now and then and saw Richard catch fleeting glimpses of her breasts and legs from the corner of her eye. She pretended not to notice. Richard was very fidgety, and he leaned toward her and whispered, "Diane, that perfume you're wearing smells incredible."

Of course that morning Diane had made sure to put on an extra dose of her best perfume for exactly that effect. She wrote on her notebook, "Thank you, I'm glad you like it. It's Chanel #5, and it cost daddy a fortune."

Richard read the note and said mockingly through his clenched teeth, "Poor daddy."

Diane smiled. Richard was falling into the trap, and she was certain that soon he would be hers. That thought gave her a warm, pulsating feeling deep inside her gut, a feeling she could not wait to assuage.

Richard did not mention that day's encounter with Diane Sorenson to Linda when they spoke on the phone that night. He didn't want her getting any ideas—at least, that's what he told himself. Of course, telling her he had invited Diane for pizza after practice the next evening—well, he didn't even want to think how he would explain that to her or how Linda would react. So, he had decided to keep the whole thing to himself because in his mind it would be a one-time thing and therefore there was nothing to talk about—or at least that's what he deluded himself to believe.

The next night when he walked out of practice, he was showered and shaved and had some clean clothes on. He felt good, but still, he was a bit nervous about meeting Diane. She was waiting for him at the locker room door, and she looked stunning. She wore a pair of tightly fitted designer jeans that had a low waist and a small diamond sparkled from the ring pierced in her belly button. Her very tight baby blue tank top made the outline of her breasts very visible and left no doubt about their size and shape. Her hair and makeup were perfect. In short, she was hot, and Richard could not help but notice.

"Hi, Richard, how was practice?" Diane gave him her best smile. Richard was perturbed by her, and he tried to hide it by answering in a matter of fact way.

"Okay. I think everyone is anxious to put the first game behind them."

"That's Saturday, isn't it?" Diane moved about in front of him, loving the effect she was having on him. Richard stared to the ground.

"Yeah, Saturday, too bad Linda can't come. She has a part-time job now, and plus she has to study." The thought that Linda would miss his first game saddened him, and mentioning her name made him feel less guilty about Diane's presence.

"Oh really, that's too bad. I'm sure she'll miss a good game." Diane was having trouble hiding her joy about Linda not being around. "But hey, Richard, the whole school will be there to cheer you on, and so will I, I promise." Diane had leaned slightly toward him and taken one of his hands and patted it in a gentle and affectionate manner. Richard blushed, but he did not remove his hand from hers right away. After a few moments he pulled it away and said, "What do you say we go eat now? I'm starving."

"Sure, Richard, me too."

They went to the favorite student hang out. It was a bar and restaurant with live bands, pool tables and a lot of rowdy students. They shared a pizza and a few beers. Diane got Richard talking about football, and he got animated and passionate while he explained to her the intricacies of the game. Diane played along and acted genuinely interested, asking questions and following his lead very well. All the time they were sitting, she directed the conversation skillfully, staying away from things like Linda, his studies, and any other subject that could have changed the mood of the moment. Richard was completely unaware of her strategies, and he talked endlessly about his favorite subject, convinced that he was having a deep and interesting conversation with her.

"So, Richard, want to shoot some pool?"

"You play pool, Diane?" Richard was surprised; Linda did not like the game and never played.

" Sure I do," she turned her back to him and walked suggestively toward the pool tables, making sure he got a good long look at her ass, which she knew looked fabulous in those jeans. She turned to him and shouted, "Loser pays the shooters."

Richard smiled as he walked to the pool table. He had eaten her with his eyes as she had walked across the room, and he was trying very hard to repress the thoughts he was having. Diane was happy because she knew that it didn't really matter who won or who lost; they were going to have shooters, no matter what. That is, he was going to have shooters. She had come in earlier and had bribed the waitress to bring Richard real shots of tequila and colored water for her. She had told the girl, "We're from the same town, and I want to play a little innocent trick on him." She had winked at the girl as she had slipped her a twenty. The waitress had obligingly played along.

They played six or seven games, and the tequila shots they ordered after every game began to hit Richard hard.

"I think we'd better call it quits, Diane. I'm not used to drinking like this."

"Okay, Richard, let's get out of here. I need some air too,"

They walked out of the bar, and Richard was a little unsteady on his feet.

"Hey, Diane, you hold up pretty good on that tequila, and you shoot a mean game of pool. I'm impressed."

"I've had a lot of practice with James. He had a pool table at home, and his father buys tequila by the case. We indulged his bar a few times, so I can handle it pretty good."

"Wow, that's great, Diane." Richard's words were becoming slurred as the tequila ripped into him. "I always thought you were a little bit, you know, fancy and precious, but you have some rock and roll in you, girl." Diane smiled and took him by the arm to help steady him. When they got to his car, she took the car keys away from him, and he protested mildly, but the reality was that he was just too drunk to drive or even wonder why she was not as drunk as he was. He sat in the passenger seat with a silly smile on his face, gazing straight ahead and bobbing to the music.

"You are quite a woman, Diane, I must admit, really quite a woman." Richard's head swayed from side to side.

"Thank you, Richard, it means a lot to me." She put her hand on his thigh and slowly ran it up and down, stopping only inches from his private parts. He leaned his head back, closed his eyes, and moaned imperceptibly. When they got to his building, Diane got out and went over to his side of the car and opened the door.

"Come on, Richard, I'll walk you up." He did not protest as she put her arm around his waist.

"I'm okay, Diane, really I'm okay," he said, but he did nothing to disengage himself from her or to stop their movement toward his apartment. Diane unlocked the door, and they let themselves in.

"Where's the bathroom, Richard?"

"Over there." He pointed in the direction of the bathroom.

Diane took a long time in the bathroom; she put on some extra perfume and took off her bra and put it in her purse. When she walked out, there was music playing, and some candles were burning. Richard was sitting on the couch; he had gotten two glasses of ice-cold water that he had placed on the table in front of him.

"Come on over and sit down, Diane." He pointed to the spot beside him on the couch. Without hesitation, she walked toward him and sat close to him, letting her hand fall on his thigh again and looking him straight into the eyes.

"I like your place, Richard," she said while looking around. He took her hand in his and pulled her gently to him, and she did not resist. Their lips met very lightly for a moment and then, they plunged into each other with all the pent-up sexual tension that the evening had produced. They devoured each other's lips, and Diane put her hand on his crotch and began to massage him slowly. He lifted her tank top off of her in a flash and began to fondle her breasts. From then on, there was no return possible. They made love three times that night. Diane was on fire; she wanted to be sure that she would leave a lasting impression.

The next morning when Richard woke up, he turned and saw Diane naked and curled up beside him. His head was thumping and he felt bad. "Oh God," he thought. "What have I done?" He looked at the clock, which indicated 10:45. "Shit, I've missed class." Diane moved a bit and opened her eyes,

"Hi, Richard, sleep well?"

"Yeah, okay, but my head feels like someone banged it with a bat." He sat on the side of the bed holding his head between his hands. Diane stroked his back. He got up slowly and put his boxers on.

"I had a course at nine. I missed a class."

"Me too, Richard, but it was worth it. You're quite a lover, you know." Diane knew how to work the male ego. Richard turned toward her and smiled, happy that she should confirm his sexual prowess.

"Well, to be honest with you, you're quite something yourself, Diane. That was exceptionally good last night." A frown came on his face. "I mean, I wish we hadn't done it, you know, because of Linda and all that, but as much as I hate to admit it, I loved every second of it." Richard turned and walked toward the kitchen, and Diane slowly got out of bed.

"Hey look, Richard," she shouted from the living room as she picked up her clothes. "You don't have to worry about me, okay? We won't tell anyone about this, and it will be our little secret, okay?" Richard sat down gloomily at the kitchen table with an orange juice in his hand.

"Thanks, Diane, I really appreciate that. That's really nice of you," he shouted back. She got dressed quickly and went to join him in the kitchen.

"Everything's cool, okay?" She leaned down and hugged him and kissed him on the lips.

"Yeah, okay."

"Don't worry, lover boy. Everything will be fine; you'll see."

"Thanks, Diane." He looked at her with sullen eyes. "So I'll see you around then, eh?"

"Yeah, you certainly will." She kissed him again and turned and began walking toward the door.

"Bye now." He watched her walk out, and she waved her hand above her head to him before closing the door behind her.

Richard put his elbows on the table and his head in his hands. He felt absolutely terrible. "I'm such a fucking prick," he said out loud. "I didn't' even call Linda last night. What am I going to say to her? Shit, shit, shit …"

While Richard was hurting and generally feeling like hell and pondering what he would tell Linda, Diane was walking away smiling and skipping happily as if to music. Everything had worked out perfectly. She could not wait to put the rest of her plans in motion. "Soon, my lovable Richard, soon our little secret will have a life of its own. I'll see to that." Diane was elated, of course. The fact that she had stolen the password to his voicemail was an added bonus. For some reason Richard had carelessly jotted it down on a piece of paper and left it on the kitchen counter. Diane had spotted the paper when she had looked for his phone while he was in the bathroom. She had wanted to be sure that his phone was shut off while they were busy with each other's bodies. She called his voicemail and punched in the code. There were two messages that Linda had left from the night before. She deleted them. "Now, the fun begins." She laughed out loud, very happy with how things were going.

Meanwhile Richard sent Linda a cheerful text and worried about when he would call her, convinced that his treason would be apparent in his voice. He decided that he would call her later that afternoon when he knew she was in class.

"Hi, baby, it's me. Sorry I didn't call you last night. I went to the pub with some of the boys, and we got a bit drunk. Well actually, quite a bit drunk. My head feels like a truck hit it. Anyway, I've got to go now. I'll call you later, okay? Love you." He hung up, aware that his message had probably sounded a bit odd.

When Linda heard his message later that day, a strange feeling came over her. Something in his voice tipped her off. He didn't sound like his usual self. She was perplexed about that and about the fact that he had obviously not listened to her messages from the night before. Later that night, after they had talked for over an hour, she was still not totally reassured. She believed Richard when he told her that he never got the messages, but it irked her not to understand why. That night, it took her a long time to fall asleep.

The next day Linda decided she would go to Richard's football game that Saturday. She would have to take time off her part-time job, but she didn't care. She felt that she had to go, that it was important. She had decided that she would surprise Richard and show up unannounced. She had to see him, to touch him, to look into his eyes; maybe then the bizarre feeling in her gut would go away. She asked Peggy to come with her, and Peggy had enthusiastically accepted. She was more than happy to be of the trip, and she had jumped up and down in the hallway when Linda had asked her about it, excited at the perspective of a party weekend.

"Yeah, great, Linda, I'd love to go with you; oh, this is going to be so much fun!"

The girls had decided that they would drive in Peggy's car and figure out sleeping arrangements when they got there. Linda was very excited but also concerned and anxious. "What the hell am I concerned about?" she kept asking herself over and over again.

Meanwhile, Richard was tortured because of his escapade with Diane. He felt bloody awful, and it was the worst he had ever felt in his life. He felt dirty and that he had cheapened his relationship with Linda, and worst, he had lied to her, and it hurt him physically every time he thought about that. He couldn't get any of these thoughts out of his head, and he walked around campus with a frown on his face.

The next day Diane came and sat beside him in class; she was very cheerful, radiant, and dressed to kill.

"Oh hi, Richard, how are you, ready for the big game Saturday?"

"Yeah, I'm ready, Diane," he said, smiling sheepishly. He turned his head and stared blankly to the floor. He felt bad just looking at her, although he was convinced Diane was a genuinely decent person who meant nobody any harm. "Hell, she had proposed to keep the whole thing a secret; I mean, how many girls would do that now?" he surmised.

"I just feel a bit awkward, about, you know, the other night. I mean to be honest, I feel like shit, with Linda and all." He brought his head up and looked toward her, a discouraged look on his face. "Don't get me wrong, Diane, it's not you, really. I had a wonderful time and you're a great person and I like you a lot, but I still feel bad."

Just then the professor began his lecture. Diane looked at him with compassion, as if she were really concerned about his turmoil, and she put her hand on his and leaned over to his ear and whispered, "its okay, Richard. I'm your friend. I really like you. I don't want you to worry, okay?"

"Okay," he whispered back. "Thanks." He squeezed her hand.

Diane leaned over again, and still whispering, she said, "Richard, let's meet later after your practice and talk things over. I'll get some food and meet you at your place and we'll talk." She stared at him with her most innocent look; there was no way he could say no to her request. He felt she really wanted to be his friend and help him through these difficult moments. His naivety was absolute.

"Sure, Diane, okay, but you don't have to you know, I'll ...."

She put a finger to his mouth, "Hush now, say no more." She leaned in closer to him and her perfume invaded his nostrils. "I want to, Richard. It's important that we talk about this and have a few laughs. Then you can concentrate on the game Saturday, nothing else matters, okay?"

"Sounds good," he whispered back, letting go of her hand and pretending to look for a page in his book.

Of course Diane prepared well for the evening. She wore a casual but very sexy outfit, and she was, as usual, impeccably done up. She checked Richard's voicemail every thirty minutes and erased a message from Linda asking him to call her back after practice. She got some takeout food and a good bottle of wine and sat in her car in front of his apartment waiting for him to come home.

Two minutes after he got home, she was at his door.

He opened the door and she strolled in with her arms full of bags and turned to face him.

"Hi, football star, I've got some food, some wine, and everything else we need." She pointed to the bags she was holding with her face. "Also, I'm in a very good mood, and I intend to cheer you up. What do you say?"

"Yeah, sounds great." Richard was a bit stunned that she was already there, but he went along. After all, he told himself, she had gone to a lot of trouble to get food and all the other stuff. He watched her walk across the room toward the kitchen and couldn't help but notice how sexy she was. Diane cleared the table and set it. She lit two candles that she had brought along for the ambiance and shut off his phone when he was in the bathroom. They ate, drank the wine, talked a lot, and had some good laughs about the silliest of things, and the atmosphere was relaxed. Richard had put on some great music, and the mood soon shifted to warm and sensual. The moment was begging for sex. Diane made the move; she literally jumped on him. He did not resist, maybe because of the wine, or the music, or the timing, or maybe just because he wanted to. They made love with the intensity of long-lost lovers. It was an impulse that they could not fight. It was stronger than them and had a life of its own, like spontaneous combustion. They fell asleep when they were finally spent, content and glued together as one.

By the time Richard got up the next morning, Diane was gone. She had an early class and had to pass by her room to get changed and pick up her school things. Richard felt bad but strangely not as bad as that first time. He took a shower and checked his voicemail; there was an irritated message from Linda asking him to call her.

"Shit," he muttered to himself as he hurriedly headed to his first class.

That Saturday morning Peggy and Linda drove toward Richard's college for the football game that afternoon. Linda still felt the strange vibe that she had been feeling for days. Richard did not call her as often, he never got her messages, he called at strange hours, and plus, his voice was different. She couldn't figure out what it was, but she was sure something was wrong. "I just hope I'm not being paranoid," she pondered.

"Hey, are you with me?" Peggy asked.

"Yes, of course I am, I was just thinking about Richard and how surprised he'll be. I can't wait to see him."

"Well, I hope he introduces me to some hunky football players. I could use some company, seeing as you'll be busy." She laughed heartily, her typical Peggy laugh, loud and loaded with life. It was contagious, and Linda broke out laughing too. The two of them got along fantastically well, so well that they could have been sisters. The laughter subsided, and Linda was staring out the car window when Peggy asked, "Hey Linda, I have a serious question to ask you, one that I've always been meaning to ask." Linda turned toward her.

"Oh yeah?"

"Yes, well, okay here it is. You are, as I am sure you are well aware of, a strikingly beautiful woman. I mean, I'm not a lesbian or anything, but you are beyond gorgeous, like real beauty, you know …"

"Thanks, Peggy, you know …" Peggy could sense that Linda was annoyed by the direction of the conversation, and she cut her off.

"Just let me finish, Linda, please?" Linda acquiesced by nodding her head, but she had a sour expression on her face.

"I mean, I see how all the guys at school, the professors, the maintenance men, and basically anything that wears pants, well anyway, I see how they devour you with their eyes. They are struck and stunned by you. Maybe you don't really notice it or you've become used to it, but I do. I have never seen anything like it, and what's fascinating is that you seem to be above it all, as if you didn't care and that it didn't matter. That is all to your merit, by the way. Anyway, here is my question. With your looks, which I repeat are exceptional, I mean, why did you not aspire to be an actress, a model, or I don't know, any career that would have put your beauty up front? It just seems to me that you were given this incredible

IAN TREMBLAY

gift at birth and that you refuse to bank on it or to use it for some reason." After a few seconds of silence, Linda answered.

"Well, first of all, Peggy, I never wanted to be an actress or model. I think that to do those jobs you have to be extremely vain and self-centered, two attributes that I do not particularly like in a person. Plus, to be an actress, well, that does require talent. It's not all about the looks, you know? Anyway, I don't have that talent, and it's just too much about the ego for my tastes. Anyway, I've always wanted to work with animals. It's been my dream and my ambition forever, so basically, I'm fulfilling my dreams. As for my looks, well, I've gotten used to how people react to my looks. I deal with it, and I try to be nice and polite to everyone. I don't abuse of my looks to get things or to make people do things I want them to do. I find that dishonest and devious. What can I say? I didn't ask to look this way. It's just the way things are. All I really want is to get an education, to have a job I love, and hopefully have a family of my own some day. I want to have a real life, one that has meaning and purpose and is filled with all the people I love. I don't think that that is too much to ask of life. What do you think, not very glamorous, eh?"

"No, not very glamorous, but who cares about glamour, eh? No, I think those are wonderful objectives, and they certainly are not too much to ask for. I'd be happy with all of that myself. Well anyway, if you ever change your mind Linda, you know, about using your looks and all that, can I be your manager?" She exploded with laughter as she said that, because she knew it was a silly thing to say, considering what Linda had just told her. Linda broke out laughing too, and they laughed to tears. Peggy turned the radio up, and they sang along to the music at the top of their lungs; it felt good to laugh and to be outrageously happy.

Two hours later they arrived outside the football stadium at Richard's college. They bought some last-minute back row seats, grabbed a few hot dogs and sodas, and settled in to watch the game. It was chilly, and the crowd was noisy and colorful. Linda felt proud when Richard was introduced to the crowd during the pre-game ceremony. She and Peggy rose to their feet and yelled at the top of their lungs. The game went well. Richard's team won, and he was the star of the game, even scoring a touchdown. Peggy and Linda were among the last people out of the stadium. After asking around, they headed toward the college pub, where they were told the team went to celebrate after a game. The pub was packed to overcapacity and was very noisy. The rock music and the clashing of glasses were mixing in with the roars of the football team and their friends who occupied the whole top section of the pub. Linda and Peggy made their way through the dense crowd. Everyone was happy and talking excitedly about the game. Room to move about was a rare commodity. Finally the girls made it up the stairs; the players were grouped in one corner and were toasting their victory loudly. Linda saw Richard in the thick of things; he was beaming with happiness, as were all of his teammates. She stopped Peggy from advancing toward them,

"Wait, let's watch them for a minute and see if he spots me." Linda smiled mischievously to Peggy. They hung there for a few minutes. People were coming up to Richard all the time to congratulate him or pat him on the back. He took all of the attention with grace, spoke to all, and shook a lot of hands. Linda felt so proud and full of love for him at that very instant that it must have sent powerful love beams across the room. Richard turned and looked in her direction. He stared at her in disbelief and smiled. He broke away from the people around him and maneuvered through the crowd to where the girls were standing.

"Baby," he shouted, "baby, baby, wow you're here."

"Surprise," she screamed, they threw themselves into each other's arms. He lifted her off the ground, spinning her and kissing her at the same time.

"Did you see the game?" Richard asked while kissing Linda over and over again.

"Yes, we got here just as it started." She held his face in her hands, kissing him back.

"Wow that is so great. God, I'm happy to see you. I love you, baby."

"Me too," she managed to say before he smothered her with another kiss.

"Hey, you two, I'm here you know. Cut it out, will you? You're embarrassing me." They turned toward Peggy.

"Sorry, Peggy, Richard, you remember Peggy?"

"Yeah, sure, hi Peggy, nice to see you."

"Hi, Richard, nice to see you too."

"Why didn't you tell me you were coming? I could have got you tickets and arranged a few things."

"Linda wanted to surprise you. I mean, all she ever talks about is Richard this, Richard that, blah, blah, blah, you know?" Peggy mimicked Linda and made a funny face.

"Oh stop it, Peggy, that's not true. Well, it is a little bit." Linda hung unto Richard's arm tightly; she was happy to have surprised him, and she felt good to be by his side again. Nothing else mattered now, and all her earlier misgivings had dissipated.

"Hey, come on you two. Let's go over to my table and I'll introduce you to some of the guys." Richard took each one of them by the arm and guided them in the direction of where he had been celebrating with his teammates. When they arrived in the midst of the celebrating team, he cupped his hands and shouted, "Silence please. A moment, guys. Hush up just for a second please." The din died down to an acceptable level, allowing Richard to speak.

"I'd like to introduce to you my girlfriend and the love of my life, Miss Linda Staunton and her charming friend, Peggy." All answered at once, some raising their glasses, "Hi, Linda, pleased to meet you. Hi, Peggy, cheers." Richard raised his arms to invoke silence again.

"Now these girls drove a few hours to come here to see us play and to surprise me, of course. I must say it is a wonderful surprise and that I am deeply touched. Let's give them a big cheer." His teammates answered his call with a healthy roar. He turned toward Linda and kissed her passionately; fueled by their passion, the shouts and cheers grew even louder.

In the pandemonium, no one seemed to notice that across the room was Diane Sorenson, leaning against a wall, her head turned toward the group and paying no attention to the guy who was trying to strike up a conversation with her. She had the team's jersey on, her cheeks were flushed, and her eyes were on fire and glued to Richard and Linda's embrace. Had her eyes been laser beams, they would have burned holes right through both of them. In a sudden and violent gesture, she shoved her glass into the hands of the solo speaking hopeful, pushed him aside, and bolted through the crowd. From the corner of his eye, Richard saw her bolt. He had noticed that she was there and was relieved to see her leave. In those few seconds he noticed that on the back of the team sweater she was wearing was his name and number.

They all had a great time, and Peggy hooked up with one of Richard's teammates, Brad. He was a very shy country boy who had been raised on a farm and he was just what Peggy needed. "Some rural recreation," she had whispered into Linda's ear with a big smile on her face.

"Richard, let's go to your place now." Linda couldn't wait to be alone with him.

"Okay, baby, but what about your friend Peggy?"

Linda turned toward Peggy, who was listening intently to Brad's monosyllabic statements. Her eyes were buried deep into his, and they were holding hands.

"Don't worry about her. She'll be okay."

"Hey, Brad." Richard motioned to him. "We're out of here. You take care of Peggy, okay?"

"Yeah sure, Richard, no problem," he blushed and smiled.

Linda waved to Peggy and shouted, "We're leaving."

Peggy waved back. "Go on, get out of here. I'm fine." She pointed with her eyes toward Brad, and the girls exchanged an understanding smile.

It took forever to get out of the pub. Everyone wanted to touch Richard, shake his hand, or congratulate him. Finally they made it outside and headed toward his apartment.

"Alone at last, my love," Richard wrapped his arms around her, and they kissed passionately. They made love slowly, very slowly, and in perfect sync; they knew each other so well. Then they talked and laughed and made love again, and the magic was still there. Richard told her about school and about football, omitting, of course, to tell her about Diane. Every time the thought of her came into his head, he felt pain and panic, and he pushed the thought as far away from his mind as he could. He didn't want to think about her when he was with Linda, and he wished he could just forget the whole thing and that it had never happened. He knew, however, that he would have to do something fast. The situation was explosive and he would have to put an end to it, hopefully without Linda finding out.

Linda told him about her courses and about Peggy and how they had become really good friends. She told him how thrilled she was about her school and how happy she was with her choice of career. She did not mention her apprehensions of late, of his calling at odd hours or the fact that he never seemed to get her messages. It would have spoiled the moment, and so she decided to save that for the next morning.

Linda woke up before Richard as day was breaking; she went to the bathroom and put on his bathrobe. She walked to the large bay window, and for a few moments she watched the spectacle of a new day beginning. She turned toward the bed. Richard was still fast asleep, and the sunlight was pouring into the room, illuminating everything. That's when she saw it, under the bed; it caught her eye because it was such a bright pink. She walked over and knelt under the bed and retrieved a sheer pink G-string. She held it in her hands and looked at it in disbelief. Her heart sank; she crumpled it in her hand and went to sit in the living room. "Maybe these were here from before," she pondered hopefully, trying to find an explanation for her find. That's when she saw them on the coffee table, two small diamond solitaires twinkling in the sunlight; beside the earrings was a small handwritten note. She picked up the note and her hand trembled as she read it.

> *Richard, darling, thank you for last night, you are the best lover I have ever had. Our secret is safe, do not worry. See you in class.*
> *Diane xxx*

A kiss had been planted on the note in lipstick. Linda began to cry, softly at first then uncontrollably, her shoulders shaking, and soon her whole body was convulsing. Richard woke up and looked in her direction. He got out of bed and went over to where she was sitting.

"Hey, baby, you're up bright and early. What's wrong? Why are you crying?" Linda did not answer. She just kept crying, and he sat down beside her. That's when he saw the G-string, the earrings, and the note, and his heart sank. Linda turned toward him; her eyes were red, and she was obviously very distraught.

"Why, Richard, why have you done this?" Richard was speechless. He picked up the note, read it, and let it drop to the floor. He looked toward Linda, his mouth agape. He was dumbfounded, but when finally he spoke, his voice was hoarse and unsteady. He confessed to everything, blaming the alcohol and his own stupidity. He cried and begged Linda for forgiveness. Linda broke down and wept uncontrollably; she was inconsolable, and each one of her heart-wrenching wails sent a shock wave through Richard's heart.

"Look, Linda, I'm so ashamed. I've been a complete idiot, and God I hate to hurt you like this, but please, Linda, please forgive me. I cannot live without you. I swear I'll die without you." Tears were pouring freely down his face too, and he was beyond himself with shame and grief.

"Jesus Christ, Richard, Diane Sorenson, of all people, that vicious, manipulative little slut," Linda's pain hissed from between her clenched teeth. She was torn between her rage and her profound sadness. Never had she felt so cheated or so betrayed in her life and by the man she loved more than anyone in the world—her Richard, her prince, the man of her dreams, the one who was encrusted in her very being and by whom and with whom she would have constructed everything. The tears kept coming in waves. The more he spoke, the less she understood and the more her heart was broken and shattered and empty.

"It was just a thing, Linda, it doesn't mean anything. I mean, it just happened. I can't explain why. I can't justify it. All I know is that I'm so bloody sorry. I didn't mean to hurt you. It breaks my heart to see you like this. I don't …" He fell silent. His words were doing nothing, and anyway, how could one explain the unexplainable? He was trapped, there was no way out, even his confession had sounded a bit off. He put his head in his hands and ran his fingers through his hair in a gesture of desperation.

"Shit, I wish all this would go away and that it had never happened. It's a bloody nightmare." Linda turned toward him.

"It won't go away, Richard. It's real, and it happened, and it hurts like hell, let me tell you." She got up and began to get dressed and gather her things.

"Oh come on, Linda, let's talk this over. I mean, give me a break here. You can't just walk out like this." He was standing behind her naked, his voice filled with panic. The thought of losing Linda scared him out of his mind. Linda remained unmoved and determined.

"I'm leaving, Richard, so get dressed and let's go find Peggy, now." The look in her eyes left no room for discussion, Richard knew that look. They did not speak in the car on the way to find Brad and Peggy, and the silence weighed heavy on both of their hearts.

When they arrived at Brad's residence, Richard got out of the car to fetch Peggy. She came out and walked toward Linda, who was still sitting in Richard's car. She was disheveled and had obviously just gotten up. She looked at Linda perplexed. They were only supposed to leave after supper that evening, and she didn't understand what Linda was doing there so early.

"What's up, Linda? Richard looks like someone died or something." Linda got out of the car.

"We have to leave right away, Peggy, please," she said in a broken voice, making an effort not to break out into tears. Her face was twisted in pain, and her eyes were swollen and red. Peggy understood that something was terribly wrong.

"Okay, Linda, if that's what you want, but I left my car in the pub parking lot last night, and so we'll have to go and pick it up." She paused, but Linda did not respond. "Okay then, let me just go in a minute to say a word to Brad and I'll be right back." She pointed in the direction of the building. Linda began to cry, and Peggy went over to where she was standing. She put her arms on Linda's shoulders, and Linda wrapped her arms around her and buried her head in her shoulder, Peggy held unto her tightly.

"Hey, whatever it is that's going on, it can't be that bad, now, can it?"

"Oh yes it is, Peggy, it's terrible. Please hurry." Tears were pouring down her face. "I really need to get out of here, Peggy. I need to get out of here now." Peggy pulled away from her, holding her by the shoulders,

"Okay, just don't move and I'll be right back, okay?" Linda wiped her tears with her forearms and nodded that she understood.

Not a word was spoken as Richard drove them to recover Peggy's car, and when they arrived in the parking lot, Peggy got out and Richard put his hand on Linda's arm just as she was opening the car door,

"Please, Linda, please, let's talk." Linda pulled her arm away,

"There's nothing to say, Richard. You've broken my heart, and right now I hate your guts, so why don't you call Diane? Maybe she'll want to talk," she shouted as she got out of the car, slamming the door shut. Quickly, she got into Peggy's car.

"Let's go, Peggy, now please." Linda's voice was laden with pain and rage, and she was on the verge of hysteria. Peggy floored the car, and they roared past Richard, who was standing beside his car with a tortured expression on his face. For the next fifteen minutes, Linda sobbed violently. She was inconsolable and miserable. Peggy drove in silence; she knew that this was not a time to talk or to ask questions.

After about an hour of driving, Linda had calmed down enough to tell Peggy what had happened.

"I'm so sorry, Linda, so very sorry." Peggy began to cry. She felt terrible for her friend whose heart had been broken by the man she loved and had trusted above all. "God, I'm sorry." She reached out and took Linda's hand. Linda squeezed her hand hard and said through her tears, "As soon as we get in we're going for a drink, Peggy. I need a drink. As a matter of fact, I need a few."

"Okay, Linda." Peggy sniffled and wiped the tears from her cheeks. "Let's do that."

So the two of them hit the pub that night and got royally drunk, especially Linda. They laughed and they cried, and although Linda tried to bury her pain in the alcohol, her heart was heavy. After they stumbled back to the dorm late that night, she cried herself to sleep, drenching her pillow with tears of desolation and her profound distress.

Richard called countless times after that day, leaving long, apologetic messages and he would text or email begging for her forgiveness, but Linda never responded. She came close to calling him a few times, dialing his number but then cutting the call off before it went through and then she would pace about her room for hours in frustration and anger, her mind in complete turmoil. Any time she thought of Diane in Richard's arms, all the hatred and rage that she had felt came up to the surface. She had been humiliated and deceived beyond redemption. The whole episode had devastated her, and now she was marked for life. She remained strong, however, and brave in spite of the bitter pain that ate at her continuously. To forgive Richard would have required more strength and courage than she possessed. After three months, he stopped calling. Somewhere deep inside her heart, she had wanted him to continue pursuing her, but at the same time, she wanted him to suffer, as much as or more than she had, and maybe one day, she told herself, she would have found it within her heart to forgive him. That, however, would have required more time and patience than the hurried imperatives and the blind certainties of youth allowed. In short, and sadly so, they were over.

Thank God for Peggy, who was a fantastic support. She was always there and was the true friend Linda desperately needed in her time of pain and sorrow. Linda cried herself to sleep most nights, and her life was a social disaster. She poured all the energy of her waking hours into her studies and her friendship with Peggy. The latter was the balm that slowly and patiently was helping to mend her shattered heart and soul.

Diane, on the other hand, was exhilarated. Unbeknownst to Richard, she had stormed out of the pub the afternoon of the game and gone to his apartment. She had a key of the door made from a double she had taken from his apartment two days before. They had been lying on the kitchen counter with a little tag that said, "Spare set of keys," and Diane had been unable to resist. With the double she had let herself into his apartment and had planted the G-string, earrings and note, not forgetting to put the spare set of keys back on the kitchen counter. The result of her work was beyond her wildest dreams.

"Oh, Richard, I'm so sorry. I mean, this wasn't supposed to happen, and it's my entire fault. I forget things all over the place, and God, the note; I left it there for you. I would never have imagined that she would see it before you. I'm so sorry. I hate myself for screwing up your life like this." She bowed her head and wiped her eyes as if she were crying. Richard took one of her hands.

"No, Diane. This is not your fault. Please don't beat yourself up about this. Things are bad enough as they are. You have been a real friend, and this is my entire fault. I mean, I should have cleaned up the apartment, you know, after the other night; but I didn't, and on the other hand, I didn't know she was coming. So, this is just not your fault, Diane, and I won't let you be so hard on yourself over this. It's just not right." Richard squeezed her hand, and she raised her head and looked at him, her eyes filled with feigned sadness and pain.

"Thank you, Richard, it means a lot to me what you just said, but I still feel bad about this. I mean, like, really bad."

"I know, Diane, but please don't, okay? It would make me feel better if I knew you weren't torturing yourself over this. It's bad enough that I am, so please not you too." Diane put her other hand on his and she leaned into his shoulder. He put an arm around her and held her tight.

"Okay, Richard, I'll try, I just want you to be happy, that's all." Diane was content; her plan had worked to perfection. Linda Staunton had given up without a fight. She closed her eyes and cuddled up against Richard's shoulder. She was beyond happy. The outcome, predictable from the get go as far as she was concerned, could not have been different. Richard Benson was hers at last, and he would be hers until she decided differently. Diane looked up to the dazed and confused Richard, who was staring blankly into space, lost in his thoughts.

"Richard, just remember that I'm here for you, whatever happens. I'm here, and I will always be here, okay?" Their eyes met.

"Thanks, Diane, that's very sweet of you." He looked away from her, his heart laden with sadness and incomprehension, completely unaware that he had been played perfectly and without an iota of a clue about how much, or how expertly.

So, life continued for Linda, as life always will, and even though she was still reeling from the end of her relationship with Richard, she kept a brave exterior. Most of all, she hated herself for having been so blind. "How could I not have seen that he was like that?" she kept asking herself. "All the time I spent with him and I saw nothing. I guess I'm just not good at figuring people out. Well, anyway, that's it for me. I've had it. No more guys till I finish school, to hell with them." Linda kept that promise to herself, and she did not get seriously involved with another guy while she was in school. She went out on a lot of double dates with Peggy and only after Peggy had really insisted, but she always remained distant with whoever was accompanying her. At the end of the evening, she would say good night and go back to her room alone. Many of those nights she would lay in bed awake for hours debating about how she had lost Richard, and she always came to the same conclusion. "He was a great guy, the best, but he was a cheater, and he broke my heart. I will never let that happen to me again." Her resolve not to get involved with anybody and not to get hurt again was absolute.

The only thing that warmed Linda's heart during those difficult years of doubt and loneliness were the cards she received from Richard on her birthday or on St. Valentine's Day. He always sent her a card on those occasions, and he had done so ever since their breakup. He kept repeating that he was sorry and that he loved her and that he always would; his words seemed genuine and sincere to Linda, but still she never answered him, although it pleased her that he still thought about her. Whenever she received one of his cards, she would spend hours staring out the residency window thinking about him. "Oh Richard, my sweet Richard, God I miss you."

Life continued for Richard too. He rode the wave of the college football star, the college's resident hero. It was a whirlwind of games and parties. Everybody wanted to know him or be his friend, and he was by far the most popular guy on campus. The team was winning because of him, and no one seemed to care that his grades were teetering on the brink of an abyss. If Diane had not helped him with his schoolwork, it would have been a disaster. She was his official girlfriend now. She walked proudly about campus with him or stood by him after games, hanging onto his arm, beaming, protecting her prize. God help any girl who came on to Richard, and the few who dared were cut down quickly and viciously by her. Richard was clearly her man now, and she would let no female come within twenty feet of him. She reigned over her territory like a tigress. Word got around that Richard was hers and hers alone.

Although Richard appeared happy on the surface, he was sad. He missed Linda terribly. Some nights when he wasn't with Diane, he drank alone in his apartment and cried. He hated himself for what had happened, and he stared for hours at the picture he had kept of Linda. It was the only one Diane had not destroyed, and he kept it well hidden from her. "Linda, my sweet, wonderful Linda, God I miss you, sweetheart." Tears rolled down his cheeks. "God I miss you."

Diane, of course, was oblivious to Richard's pain, as she was to anybody's pain or needs. The only needs that counted for her were her own. For her, things were going exceptionally well, Richard Benson, the school's quarterback and resident hero was her boyfriend. She organized things so that she fit into his schedule. She was always there at the right time and had things figured out to the smallest detail. Richard went along. He got used to her being there always right on cue. He firmly believed she was a true friend who was his biggest supporter and who only wanted what was good for him.

The truth was that he did not have the strength or the wits to stand up to Diane Sorenson, and she was always miles ahead of him on everything. She directed and controlled his life without him really noticing. Everything in Diane's life was calculated and organized; nothing was left to chance or improvisation. She was not, as Richard believed, fitting into his life, but he was fitting into hers. For Diane, Richard was a moveable part. He occupied the moments of her life that she had decided were important for her. She directed everything to fit perfectly into her meticulously planned existence. Diane was brilliant, beautiful, and sexy; plus, she had rich parents who spoiled her and gave her anything she wanted. What she could not get through conniving or charm, she could always try to buy. She was, as she liked to say, "A vicious little bitch," who would stop at nothing to get what she wanted. She was also an excellent student, with stellar grades, and was very involved in the schools' political and social activities.

Her number-one priority, though, was to make sure that Richard lacked of nothing, that he had what he needed before he even knew he needed it—especially sex. There was always a lot of that. Diane had learned very young the power of sex over men, and she used it to the extreme. The complacent and unsuspecting Richard went along; making no effort to understand what was going on. The relationship was comfortable and the sex was great and he admired Diane's strength and energy. He liked how she took care of everything; it made him feel important and loved. He could not, however, no matter how hard he tired, get Linda out of his mind. Linda had been the love of his life, the woman he had wanted to marry and to have children with. Now she was gone forever, and he couldn't get over it, no matter how much sex and attention Diane poured on him. He kept his heart's discontent to himself, however, concentrating on football and school; yet, buried in the bottom of his heart and tattooed to its' very walls was the inscription, "Linda Staunton, forever."

The school year came and went. Linda's world had revolved around school and Peggy and a few other friends she had made on campus. She was in great spirits when she left to spend the summer with her family at home. She was excited and buoyant at the promise that the coming months held; she couldn't wait to spend time with her brother and sisters and her mother and grandparents.

In the second week she was home, she saw Richard again by accident at the shopping mall. She had gone shopping with her mother and her younger brother Derek when she saw Richard and Diane pass hand in hand in front of the store they were in. They did not see Linda, as they were not looking that way. It had given Linda an electroshock to the heart to see them, jolting her, and she had felt her knees weaken and had momentarily felt sick to her stomach and had turned pale. Her mother had turned to talk to her just then, and noticing her change of composure, she had come up to her and taken one of her arms.

"Linda, are you okay? You seem pale all of sudden."
She put her hand on Linda's forehead to check for fever.

"I'm okay, Mom, it's nothing. I'm fine. I'm just tired from the school year and all that. I'm fine, really." Linda's color had returned a bit. She smiled to her mother, who, reassured, went back to her shopping. Linda stared blankly out the store window where she had just seen Richard and Diane pass. It was the first time she had ever seen them together. All the pain of her break up with Richard came rushing back. She remembered it well now, and it was as if it had just happened, and it hurt—it hurt like hell.

The summer flew by, and soon it was time to go back to school. Linda threw herself into her studies; she got top marks and was an honors student. With Peggy she got involved in some humanitarian causes and helped on weekends at a local shelter for battered women. True to her promise to herself, she did not get involved in a serious relationship, and it stayed that way for the remaining years she was in school. She lived only for her studies, her volunteer work, her visits home for the holidays, and summer vacations. She and Peggy had become inseparable and they did everything together. When they were away from each other during the summer, they would talk for hours on the phone. The best part of going back to school in September for Linda was the prospect of being with Peggy again. She had become like another sister to her. Their friendship was pure and profound, and nothing could have altered that. All in all, the years at school were good years for Linda. She was happy and excited about the future. Everything seemed possible, and although her heart was still scarred from her break up with Richard, the years seemed to have eased the pain, and the hurt she had suffered subsided. She had been slowly healing and her heart was opening up again, and life was beckoning her with open arms.

Chapter 2

TRAGEDY

Linda and Peggy both finished school with top honors, and they were among the five best students of their graduating class. Graduation day was magical for both of them. Linda's mother was there, and so were her grandmother, grandfather, brother, and two sisters. All of Peggy's family was there too. Everyone was thrilled by the girls' accomplishments and the anticipation of an exciting future for them. Joy filled the air and dominated the brilliant summer day. They took pictures, cried, kissed, shook hands, and everyone seemed to be talking at the same time; it was a day that would be crystallized in the memory of all those who were there for many years to come. Linda's mother was particularly happy and proud of her daughter.

"Mom, I'm so excited I've graduated. I can hardly believe it. Thank you, Mom. Thank you for everything you've done for me. I know how much you sacrificed so this day could happen. This is your day too, Mom." Linda took her mother in her arms, and they hugged for a long time, each shedding a silent tear.

"Oh come on, Linda, I only did what I had to do. No, this is your day, Linda, and I'm really proud of you." She wiped her tears with a tissue and smiled, looking at her daughter, beaming. "Just look at you, a grown woman, beautiful and talented and with a brand new future in front of you." They stood facing each other holding hands, each filled to overcapacity with the emotions of the day.

"You know, Mom, what you did for us was extraordinary. I mean, you raised four children singlehandedly. Now that is a real achievement in my book. You are my hero, Mom, a real life hero, and you are the person I admire the most in the world, and I love you very, very much." Linda took her mother in her arms again and wrapped her arms around her.

"Oh hush now, you'll make me cry again."

Peggy and Linda had both been hired to work in the same clinic. They had planned it that way. Since neither of them was involved in a serious relationship, they had decided to stay together for a while. It had been easy to arrange; as top-notch graduates, they had gotten many offers from all over the country. The city they were going to would be a new one for both of them. They had only been there once to visit the clinic and for their job interviews. The clinic was a large, well-run operation with a large staff. The corporation that owned the clinic owned forty other clinics across the country. The pay would be good, and there were many perks and fringe benefits. The HR person who had recruited them had insisted, "We take good care of our people here, and we do everything we can to make sure that they are happy with us. We choose the most talented and promising people, and we do everything we can to keep them." Linda and Peggy had walked away from the interview excited at the prospect of working there. They had found a nice sunlit apartment not too far from where they would work, and they had rented it. Everything was set. They had jobs waiting for them and a place to stay, and they were both impatient to start work and to move in.

The girls had taken a month off after graduation to go home before moving and starting to work. Linda was glad to be home and to spend some time with her family. She loved the family meals when they all sat down and ate together. Even though her mother had very limited means, there was always enough of everything, and the food was great. Linda promised herself that she would help her mother as soon as she made a bit of money. Her brother and sisters all had part-time jobs now, so everyone pitched in and things were not as bad as before. There was one thing that they did have plenty of and that was the love they had for each other. Love was the single common denominator of the Staunton household. It had always been and was inherent to everything they thought, did, or said. Linda was very grateful for the blessing of having such a truly loving and caring family.

One day during that month Linda stopped by a coffee shop to buy a latte. As she was waiting for her order, a girl of about her age came up to her.

"Hi, Linda, remember me?" Linda looked at her, but did not recognize the girl.

"I'm sorry, no."

"I'm Debbie, Debbie Stewart, you know? I used to wear glasses and had pimples all over my face." Linda was still looking at her with a questioning look. "Oh, and I used to hang out with Diane Sorenson." She made an expression like, "not a great reference, I know, but maybe it will ring a bell."

"Oh yes, I remember you. I'm sorry it's been a few years now." Linda smiled; the mention of Diane's name did not bother her as much as it used to.

"Don't worry about it, Linda, it happens all the time. You know the hair, the contacts, no more pimples, it changes a person. So, how have you been? I heard that you graduated. Congratulations."

"Thanks, Debbie, yeah I did, and I've already got a job and an apartment. I'll be leaving next week. And you?"

"Well, I'll be graduating next year, and I'm getting married to Sidney in August. We met at college. Life is good. I can't complain."

"Good for you." Linda's attention turned to her order, which was ready; she was glad to get out of there. To spend any more time than she had to with a friend of Diane Sorenson's was not her idea of time well spent.

As if she read Linda's mind, Debbie said, "Hey, Linda, just to be clear, me and Diane haven't spoken in years, and I'm certainly not one of her friends anymore. I just said that so you would remember me. Well anyway, now that we've met, there is something that I would like to share with you about her and your ex, Richard. I think there are certain things that you should know. Do you have time for a coffee before you leave?" The mention of Richard's name piqued Linda's interest. Her curiosity got the better of her, and she definitely wanted to hear what Debbie had to say. Without wanting to appear too interested, she replied, "Sure, why not. Let's have coffee. I'm staying at my mom's. Here, take my number." Linda began to walk toward the door and turned around before stepping out. "I'm free tomorrow if you want Debbie?"

"Yeah, tomorrow would be great Linda. I'll call you."

"Ok then, see you tomorrow." Linda was perplexed as she walked out; she wondered what Debbie had to say to her. Mostly, though, it was the mention of Richard's name that moved her and caused an uneasy stirring in her stomach. Even after all this time, it still did that to her.

The next day Linda met Debbie at Larry's Diner. They used to hang out there when they were teens. Debbie was already there with a coffee in front of her.

"Hi, Linda, how are you?"

"I'm good, thanks, and you?"

"Never been better, thanks. Would you like something?" Debbie motioned to the waitress to come over, and Linda ordered a tea. They talked about college and their high school days for a while, and then Debbie cleared her throat.

"So, okay, Linda, here's the story I wanted to tell you about Diane and Richard. Prepare yourself, because it's not pretty. Well, the first year I went to college I still hung out with Diane Sorenson, and as you know, she ended up going out with Richard, your ex, before the Christmas break." Linda nodded, sipping her tea, saying nothing. "Well, some time later in that school year, we had a girls' night out, like, you know, five or six girls, dinner, drinks, and girl talk, that kind of night. So anyway, I sat beside Diane that night at dinner, and with Diane, as you know, you only speak about what interests Diane, so naturally the subject of Richard kind of came up. Anyway, by then we all had had quite a bit to drink, and everyone was more or less drunk. So out of the blue, Diane turns to me and asks me, "Hey, Debbie, want to know how I stole Richard from that little clueless bitch Linda Staunton?' Sorry about the language, but those were her words," Linda motioned with her hands that it was okay.

"Of course, that was not really a question. Diane had decided that she would tell me this story, whether I was interested to hear it or not." Debbie went on to tell Linda about how Diane had boasted to her about trapping Richard. "She told me how she had planned everything to the smallest detail and called Richard a moron and an idiot for having fallen so easily and how she had found out the password for his voicemail and had a lot of fun erasing the messages you left him. Also, that she had stolen his spare set of keys and had used them to plant stuff in his apartment a few hours before you showed up there with him. The whole time she told me this Linda, she laughed; she reveled in it and thought it was hilarious. Then she went on and on about how stupid you and Richard had been, I'm sorry to say that, but those were her words. So that's the story, Linda. I'm sure that today it makes no difference in your life, but I'm glad I met you and to be able to share this with you. I just think that it's fair that you know how mean she was to both of you and what a terrible person she had been."

Linda looked at her; her heart was filled with mixed emotions and her mind was flooded with anger by what she had just heard.

"Thanks, Debbie. Well, that's certainly not what I expected you would be telling me, wow! How can somebody be so mean, Debbie? That's something I just can't understand."

"I think she's mean inside, Linda, like really mean and angry. It's her ego. It's bigger than her and controls her life completely. She is so full of herself that even the slightest setback drives her crazy, and I think that deep down inside, she's a very unhappy person."

"Yeah, I guess you're right. You know, in a way, I feel sorry for her. She has to live with herself." There was an awkward silence. "So tell me, Debbie, what happened between you and her? Why did you stop being friends?"

"Well, nothing really, oh, something trivial, I argued with her about clothes or something of that nature, and that was it. Diane decided I was out, to be shunned and ignored. I didn't mind that much and I made some real friends for a change. I concentrated on my studies and eventually met Sidney. So, in a way, things worked out okay I guess. As for Diane, well, all I can say is that in retrospect, she was an evil little bitch; excuse the language Linda, but there is no other way to say it. I'm really sorry she hurt you and split you and Richard up. That was mean and just not right."

Linda smiled. "Its okay, Debbie, that's all ancient history now. As far as I'm concerned, Diane Sorenson is dead. I've wiped her from my memory." Shortly after that the girls left. They said good-bye and wished each other good luck. Although she did not let it show, what Debbie had revealed to Linda bothered her a lot. All the old hurt and pain came back to her, and it churned inside her gut and burned inside her head. She walked back home in silence, torn between her rage and sadness and fighting hard to hold back her tears.

Too soon the time came for Linda to leave. This departure was different than leaving for school and it wasn't just because she was traveling further. No, there was something more permanent about this move. Everyone was there to wish her off; all promised to visit soon and wished her the best. Linda had mixed emotions as she settled into her seat for the long train ride, a ride to a new city, a new job, a new apartment, and a new life with her friend Peggy. The thought of Peggy made her smile and cheered her up a bit. Peggy always had that effect on her.

Settling in went really well. Linda and Peggy were enthusiastic about everything. They had taken their first week together to set up their apartment. They cleaned, painted, and decorated, and in no time, their little nest was organized. The furniture was old, but it was in good shape and clean; the girls had added a little personal touch everywhere, not with expensive ideas but with creative ones. In the living room they had covered the sofa and chairs with matching bright tissues, and in the kitchen they had painted the chairs and the table a light shade of pink. For every room and for every wall they had added an object or a color that gave it that extra touch; the touch of warmth and sincerity, igniting every square inch of their cozy abode with the incandescence and promise of youth.

The plumbing and lighting were a bit dated, but everything worked, and the building superintendent had been really helpful and nice. Mr. Delvechio had immediately liked them; he was an older gentleman of seventy or so, but in great shape and very lively and talkative. He was polite, and his clothes were well kept. He spoke with a heavy accent, and he told them he had emigrated from Hungary with his parents after the war when he was still a boy. When the girls had come to give Mr. Delvechio their first month's rent, he had insisted they sit down and have tea with him and his wife.

"Sixty-four years I've been in this country, and it seems like only yesterday. I've never been back there, you know, to Hungary. I'm told things have changed now, but me and Edna, we're too old to go back there. Here is our home now, and here is where we'll be buried." He turned toward his wife and tapped her hand gently; she acquiesced by nodding her head and smiling. "As for you two, well, you're both in a new city where you know no one, just like Edna and I when we were children. So, we'll watch over you and this will be your home and you'll be safe here." He turned to his wife, who smiled approvingly. "Look at these two, Edna, so young, so beautiful, all their future in front of them, neither of them married. Can you believe that? Wait and see, Edna, men will come knocking on that door very soon. Mark my words, a second lock I'll have to install to keep them out, Edna. Believe me, I know these things." His wife shrugged and said nothing; after forty-seven years of marriage, Edna had learned the virtues of silence. The girls were flattered by the Delvechios, who acted with them more like benevolent grandparents than landlords. Once they finished their tea, they got up to leave, but only after having answered many questions about their families, their jobs, why they were not married, and so on. When they were out of ear's reach of the first-floor apartment of the Delvechios, Linda looked at Peggy and they both broke out laughing, exchanging knowing looks.

"Wow, aren't they something, eh, Peggy?"

"Oh, they're so sweet and caring. I love them. It's like having family in the building."

"Yeah, they're great. I love them too." The girls had reached their door, and they let themselves into their apartment. They slouched onto their sofa, content with their new home and excited about the next day, which would be their first day of work.

They woke up at seven the next morning. Peggy got breakfast ready, and they had cereals and berries and toast with some jam that Linda's grandmother had made.

"So I guess this is it, Linda. Today we enter the adult world." Peggy's mouth was full, and she spoke from the side of her mouth.

"Yup, this is the real thing, Peggy. God, I'm excited." Linda was nervous. The whole idea of her first real job felt good but strange at the same time. She had butterflies in her stomach and kept checking her watch even though they had all the time in the world. Peggy, on the other hand, seemed totally relaxed and completely unstressed; she was calmly finishing off the toast and jam and in no hurry to get ready. In a way, that fundamental difference in their characters was one of the reasons why they had become such great friends.

At eight-thirty they met Derek Wesley, the general manager of the clinic; he greeted them politely and asked them to sit down. He was a small, serious, bespectacled man of about fifty who sat very upright behind his desk.

"Welcome, ladies, I'm glad that you have decided to come and work at this clinic and for this company. Now, let me explain to you a little bit how things work around here." He then went into a lengthy explanation about company policies, the clinic, their work schedules, and how they were expected to perform in their new work environment.

"You see, this is a very upscale clinic, upscale in the sense that our customers are very well to do people and they cherish their pets greatly. They want their pets pampered as much as they themselves like to be pampered. We believe in customer service here. We are well known for that. It is important that you keep that in mind, as you are now both part of my team." He paused and let his words sink in. Linda spoke for both of them.

"Thank you, Mr. Wesley. We are very happy to be here, sir. We know the company has a fine reputation, and we are proud to be part of your team. As a matter of fact, we can't wait to get started." Linda looked toward Peggy, who shook her head vigorously in a sign of approval. Wesley was satisfied. He knew both of them had finished among the top of their class and that they had passed all the human resources' tests and the strict company screening process with flying colors. They would be serious and dedicated employees, he was sure of that. He did, however, keep a severe look on his face. After all, he was the boss, and he believed that he had to instill a firm link of authority with any new arrivals. When the meeting was over, Derek Wesley picked up the phone.

"Maria, could you ask Jeff Peterson to come to my office please?" He put the phone back down. "Now, Linda and Peggy, I have asked Jeff Peterson, one of our top veterinarians, to show you around the facility and to introduce you to everyone. He will also give you your schedules and answer any questions you might have. Is this all clear so far? Do you have any questions?" The girls looked at each other.

"No sir, no questions, everything's fine." Linda answered for both of them again; Peggy acquiesced by nodding her head. There was a knock on the door.

"Come in," Wesley said with a tint of authority.

Jeff Peterson walked in; he was a tall and slender man of about thirty, with a soft and sensitive manner about him. Rising from his chair, Wesley introduced the girls to him. He shook their hands and seemed genuinely pleased to meet them. The girls couldn't help but notice that Jeff Peterson was a very good-looking man. His hair was ash blonde, and his green eyes had a mischievous twinkle in them.

"Peggy, Linda, what do you say we get out of Mr. Wesley's hair?" Both girls readily agreed and were more than glad to get away from the pontificating and stiff Derek Wesley.

"Yeah sure, thank you, Mr. Wesley, have a nice day, sir." Linda got up, and Peggy did the same. They walked out with Jeff Peterson in tow.

Jeff showed them around and introduced them to everyone, and he insisted they call him by his first name. He was lively and had a good sense of humor. He asked them about school and about where they were from and about their families. He was a good communicator, and he obviously loved his work very much by the way he talked about it. Everyone they met seemed to like him. He was pleasant and polite with all, and the girls got the impression that he was genuine and sincere. They liked him a lot, and after the slightly suffocating interview with Derek Wesley, his humanity was refreshing. At the end of the tour, he gave them their schedules, and as expected, they got nights and weekends.

"Hey look, I did nights and weekends for two years and I survived," he said as he handed them their schedules with a smile.

"Oh, we don't mind, Mr., I mean Jeff. We just can't wait to start, and nights and weekends are fine." Linda was excited and was elated about the clinic. It was new and had all the most modern equipment and she was impressed by the people they had met so far. They all seemed so friendly and professional to her.

"Yeah, let's hear it for nights and weekends," Peggy added, smiling radiantly. She felt as enthusiastic about the place as Linda.

Jeff Peterson was amused by the two young recruits; he liked their eagerness and their freshness. He also couldn't help but notice how astoundingly beautiful Linda Staunton was and that she wasn't wearing an engagement ring. The bachelor in him couldn't help but hope that there was no boyfriend in the picture.

"So tell me, ladies, where is this fantastic apartment you have been telling me about?"

"It's about twenty minutes away, on 32nd street near Clearview Avenue. Do you see where that is?" Linda looked at him; she liked his soft manner and his attentiveness to what they said. She also noticed that he wore no wedding ring, and she knew that she and Peggy would talk about that later.

"Yeah sure, I know where that is. Well anyway, if you ever do a housewarming, I want to be invited. Is that a deal?" The girls looked at each other and smiled.

"Yeah, that's a deal," Linda said, even though a housewarming was not something she and Peggy had thought about or discussed.

"Do you know anyone else in this city?" he asked, amused.

The girls looked at each other and shrugged,

"You mean besides you?" Peggy asked.

"Yes, besides me." He smiled.

"Well, we know Mr. Wesley," she replied while keeping a straight face.

They all broke out laughing.

"With all due respect, I don't think you want to go there. I'll tell you what, if you do get something organized, I'll bring a few friends, girls, guys, and we'll get you started on the social side of things. What do you say?"

"Yeah sure, sounds great. Give us a bit of time to get our bearings, and we'll give you a nod. After all, you're the first one on our very short list." Linda smiled. She had answered spontaneously without even looking at Peggy. They all laughed again, and Peggy felt the vibe that was passing between them.

"So that's it for now, ladies. I have got to get back to work, and I guess I'll be seeing you around. Oh, and once again, welcome aboard." He smiled, shook both their hands, and trotted down the corridor.

"He's cute," Peggy said once he was out of ear reach.

"Yeah, he's nice," Linda answered in a much too matter of fact way. "You know what, Peggy? I think I'm going to like working here." Peggy ignored Linda's comment; she would not be deterred from talking about Jeff Peterson.

"Did you notice, Linda?"

"Notice what."

"Mr. Peterson, Jeff, he doesn't wear a wedding ring."

"So what, maybe he's gay. Who cares?"

"No way he's gay, Linda, did you see how he was looking at you? He was devouring you, and I mean like big time."

"Oh come on, Peggy, enough already. He was just being nice, that's all."

"Linda, don't play dumb with me, okay? That guy was really taken by you, and I think you like him too. Hey look, I felt the vibe between you too. It was pretty obvious."

"Well, I don't know about that, and you know what? I don't care; I came here to work and not to get into a relationship. I'm in no hurry to get involved with someone and especially someone I work with."

"Oh come on, Linda, so you've been burned by love, big deal. I mean, look at me and my string of assholes and losers. I haven't given up. I just know there's a Mr. Right out there for me, I just haven't found him yet, that's all."

Okay, Peggy, so be it. All I'm saying is slow down here, this is our first day, let's not get ahead of ourselves, okay? As for Jeff Peterson, well, we just met the guy, and he's a professional colleague of ours, remember that."

"Yeah okay, Linda, but he was flirting with you."

"He was not."

"Yes he was.

"No he wasn't."

"Well okay, then, but he's cute." Linda turned toward her and smiled.

"Okay, Peggy, he's cute. Are you happy now?"

"Yes, I'm happy," she said and smiled.

"He likes you, I'm sure."

"No he doesn't."

"Yes he does." Peggy bumped Linda with her shoulder, and they both broke out laughing.

They quickly got into the clinics routine, and everyone fell in love with them. In no time they had made friends amongst the personnel, the customers, and of course, the pets. Linda loved the animals. She felt she had a connection with

RICH HOMELESS BROKEN BUT BEAUTIFUL

them. She was especially good with the dogs, and they seemed to be naturally attracted to her. The night and weekend shifts didn't bother them at all, and since they were on the same schedule, they traveled to work and did the chores and the shopping together. As for men—well, there was not really time for that in the first three months. Of course, when they went out, guys hit on them all the time, especially Linda. But nothing of any importance occurred; the girls were just too busy with their new jobs to even seriously think about guys or relationships. Linda liked Jeff Peterson more and more, even though she hated to admit it that to herself. She was attracted to him, and she could tell that it was the same thing for him. Anytime they met she could feel it. It was like electricity arcing from one to other. They both would have denied it if someone had asked, but it was there, drawing them to one another, inexorably, and a little more so every day.

One evening as Linda came into work, she ran into him. Of course she did not know that Jeff always stayed a bit longer after work so he could run into her.

"Hi, Linda, how are things?" He asked, flashing his best smile.

"Oh hi, Jeff, fine, thank you. Everything is really great. I love the place, and everyone is really nice. It's exactly what I had hoped it would be and more and how about yourself, you good?"

"Yeah, I'm good, no complaints. Oh, by the way, I'm still waiting for that invitation." Linda looked at him with a puzzled expression.

"Invitation?" she repeated.

"Yeah, you know, to the housewarming party. You guys said you might do something."

"Oh yeah, well Peggy and I talked about it only yesterday." For some reason she lied, which was so unlike her, and there was an awkward silence.

"Well?" Jeff looked at her amused, waiting for the rest.

"I'm sorry; I just had a blank there." Linda fidgeted in place; she was nervous. "Yes, well, we thought that maybe Friday in two weeks would be good. We are both off that night," she said hesitantly.

"Great, am I still invited?"

"Yes, of course you are."

"Okay then, it's settled. I'll bring a few friends, if that's still okay. You know, seeing as you don't have any," his attempt to make a joke fell flat and Linda stared at him blankly for a moment, lost in her thoughts.

"Are you sure about this, Linda?" He asked in a more serious tone.

"Yeah absolutely," she snapped out of her reverie. "I just have to check with Peggy that's all." She smiled.

"Fine then, I look forward to it. I have to be off now, Linda. I'll see you around then."

"Yeah you too Jeff … thanks."

Linda just stood there in shock; the truth was she hadn't even talked to Peggy about doing the housewarming Friday in two weeks. "Why did I just say that, and why did I thank him, because he talked to me? I'm such a loser with men. It's pathetic." With those thoughts swirling in her head, she hurried to find Peggy before Jeff ran into her and talked to her about his invitation. It was easy convincing Peggy. She had been harassing Linda for weeks about doing a housewarming party.

"So it's settled. Friday in two weeks then, great," Peggy squealed with delight.

She immediately began to prepare for the party with enthusiasm. She invited people from work and a few guys they met regularly at a bar they went to after work from time to time. Linda, on the other hand, was filled with apprehensions and nervous about having Jeff Peterson in her home, but she grudgingly went along with the preparations.

Jeff was the last to arrive that Friday; he brought a magnificent bouquet of flowers and two bottles of Italian wine. Linda opened the door for him.

"Hello, Linda. Here, these are for both of you." He handed Linda the flowers and kissed her on both cheeks. "You look great, by the way." Linda smiled; she was pleased with the compliment and happy to see him.

"Thank you, Jeff. The flowers are awesome. Please, come on in." She leaned into the door to let him pass. He walked around the room and said hello to everyone, taking the time to listen and chat up those he did not know. It was a mellow, smooth-running party. The air was cool from the open windows, and the music was just right, not too loud and not too invasive. The conversations flowed, and all were happy to be there and were enjoying the evening. Linda and Peggy were happy. They had all these new people in their lives, and they loved their new home and their new jobs, and it just felt good to be alive.

"So, Linda Staunton," Jeff had finally cornered her in the living room, not that Linda had been avoiding him, but maybe a little. "Tell me about yourself. You are a very mysterious woman, you know."

"Me mysterious? No, I'm just an ordinary girl who's very lucky and very happy with her life at this moment. That's it, nothing else." Linda became nervous when he came close to her. His physical presence lit up every nerve end in her body.

"Oh come on, Linda, you're a magnificent and extremely attractive woman with no visible boyfriend in the picture," Jeff looked around the room to emphasize his point, "and that, is mysterious … unless," he hesitated and looked toward Linda, not finishing his sentence.

"Unless what?" Linda looked at him, perplexed.

"Well," he hesitated, "don't mind me asking, Linda, but something just dawned on me. Are you and Peggy, you know, like, together?" he said while pointing his eyes and fingers in her direction then Peggy's. Linda exploded with laughter.

"No, Jeff, we're not together, really, wow. Look, it's very simple; I've had some really bad experiences with love—well, really one bad experience—and I'm still a bit fragile from that. Plus, I promised myself that I would finish my school, get settled into a good job, and then I would see about relationships. I mean, basically that's it. No mystery there." Jeff laughed whole-heartedly, and Linda joined in.

"My God, how could I have thought that? Look, I'm really sorry, and I hope I haven't offended you."

"No, of course not, I understand why you could have thought that. I mean, here we are, two girls living together and neither has a boyfriend, so it's more than possible in this day and age. I hope that doesn't disappoint you too much," Linda added with a taint of sarcasm.

"No, of course not, are you mad? Believe me, I'm really happy that you're not gay, Linda. That would have really disappointed me." He smiled at her and took a sip of his wine.

"And you?" Linda looked him straight in the eyes.

"And me what?" He looked at her with a clueless expression on his face.

"Well, are you gay? Is that why you thought that about me and Peggy?" Jeff's eyes opened wide, and he had a look of disbelief on his face. Pointing to himself he said, "Me? No, of course not, Linda, I'm not gay, as a matter of fact I'm nowhere near gay. Look, it's really very simple; I've had some unfortunate experiences with love recently, and I'm still reeling from that, so I decided to remain a bachelor until I found someone that I really believe I could have a long-term relationship with."

"Touché," Linda smiled at the reference he had made to her own answer; the ice had been broken between them and they had actually talked about something other than work. They sat on the sofa and began to chat, talking for a few hours, exchanging life stories and laughing a lot. They seemed unaware of the other people around them, and Linda was surprised how much she opened up to him and him to her. Jeff was compassionate and understanding and she felt warm and comfortable and protected sitting beside him. He was also a good listener and was quick to pick up on things, and that pleased her a lot. It felt right to be in his company, and Linda had not felt like that about someone since Richard.

Soon the party winded down and everybody left. Jeff was the last to go. Peggy had gone to bed or passed out, and Jeff and Linda were still sitting on the sofa. He took one of her hands, and she stiffened, but she did not remove her hand from his.

"I really like you a lot, Linda. I mean, like in an important way." Linda began to protest, but he put a finger to her lips.

"Just listen, please. I'm not an easy guy. I don't sleep around, and I've been waiting a long time to find someone like you, and now you're here. I just can't ignore what I feel any longer. I have to share this with you. It's exploding inside of me." He put a hand on his chest to indicate his heart. Linda felt uncomfortable. Her eyes went from him to the floor, and she was torn between her own feelings for him and her fear of falling in love again.

"I like you too, Jeff, but we work together, and I think it would be a mistake and confuse things for both of us."

"I knew you would say that, Linda, and I understand. I'm not pressuring you or anything, and I'm not in a hurry, so please take your time to think this out. You're a rare woman, Linda, and I will wait for you. I'll do anything for you; I'll change jobs if I have to." They were close, inches apart, and he was still holding her hand, and she did nothing to disengage it. Their eyes locked. He leaned slowly forward and kissed her gently on the lips. She closed her eyes, and he slowly pulled her in his direction. Their lips met again and they took each other's mouth hungrily, releasing through their embrace all the pent-up passion of the past months. Linda threw her arms around him and abandoned herself in the kiss; she began to breathe heavily and felt a tingle in her gut. The floodgates of love were wide open, and her whole being was ignited and on fire. She caught herself just in time and put her hands on Jeff's shoulders, pushing him away gently. She was flushed and excited and had trouble regaining her composure.

"Please, Jeff, please stop."

She took his hands in hers and looked him in the eyes. Linda was not ready to go any further; she had not made love to a man for a long time and was afraid of what might happen.

"I want so much to be with you, Jeff, but, I'm not ready yet, so please go. Go before things happen, please." Jeff heard the words, but he also saw what her eyes were saying. He smiled and kissed her hands.

"It's okay. Linda, there's no hurry. Let's take our time."

Linda smiled. "Thank you. Thank you for understanding."

He stood up. "Thanks for everything, Linda, it was a great evening. I had a wonderful time." Linda stood up and walked with him toward the door. He turned before going out the door and passed his hand delicately through her hair.

"Sweet dreams, Linda. I'll see you soon." He leaned over and kissed her forehead and then brushed his lips with hers. Linda closed her eyes and inhaled his odor. She opened them again, and he was inches away. His eyes were smiling, and he was happy and buoyant with the thought of them being together again soon.

"Sweet dreams too," Linda whispered. He let go of her hand and walked away. He turned in the stairs and blew her a silent kiss. She waited for him to have disappeared in the stairwell and then closed the door of her apartment. She leaned her back on the door and let out a long languorous sigh, the kind of sigh that comes from deep inside a person where the roots of unfulfilled love reside. She went to sit on the couch and thought for a long time about what had just happened. She was happy but worried. She wanted a man in her life, a man like him. He was everything she dreamed of, but she was scared of being hurt again and was eaten by doubt and uncertainty. With those conflicting emotions still twirling in her mind, she got up and slowly made her way to her bedroom.

The next day was a day Linda Staunton cannot remember, but also a day she can never forget. Her mother and Peggy filled in the blanks for her later, much later. What happened on that day at precisely 4:37 p.m., according to the police report, changed her life forever.

She had been in a hurry and was late for work. She had been running to catch her bus and never saw the car that hit her. To this day, she cannot remember that moment. Actually, two cars hit Linda Staunton that day. The first one hurled her in the air, and she landed seventy feet away in the middle of the street. Then another car coming in the opposite direction had slammed into her fallen body and dragged her on the pavement. When it finally came to a stop, another car rear-ended it, and they both exploded into flames. The flames had engulfed both vehicles, and two bystanders, at the risk of their own lives, had miraculously pulled Linda's mangled and burned body from beneath the flaming vehicles.

She had been rushed to the hospital in critical condition. Linda's body had been brutally crushed and burned. She had suffered multiple fractures to just about every bone in her body, and her face had been charred beyond recognition. Her chest and neck were severely burned, and she was in shock. In those first few hours, the doctors did not nourish much hope that she would survive. Peggy had been the first to arrive; Linda was in the operating room when she got there. She had waited around nervously, pacing about and breaking into tears all the time. No one would or could tell her exactly how Linda was doing, but she understood the words "critical and life-threatening injuries" that the head nurse had pronounced at the desk. "The doctor will come and see you as soon as he gets out of the operating room, miss. Please be patient and wait for him in the waiting room. That's all I can tell you for now, I'm sorry." So, Peggy had waited, for what had seemed to her an interminable number of hours. Finally the doctor showed up. He still had his scrubs on and was obviously coming straight from the operating theatre. He was a lanky, handsome man of about fifty, with graying temples and gentle blue eyes. Peggy stood up when he walked up to her.

"Hi, I'm Dr. Hall. Are you next of kin to Miss Staunton?" His voice was soft, and he spoke slowly, in a reassuring and comforting manner.

"No, I'm her roommate. Her mother lives out of town. How is she?" Peggy was in a state of extreme anxiety.

"Please sit down, will you?" He took Peggy's arm and directed her toward a couch. His fingers were long and delicate, and his hand was warm. He sat down in front of her and looked at her; his eyes emanated compassion and understanding. His very presence had a calming effect on Peggy.

"Okay, miss?"

"Peggy."

"Well, Peggy, here is the situation. Your friend has had a horrific accident, and the fact that she is still alive as we speak is miraculous. She is very strong. I'd say that her chances of surviving the next forty-eight hours are fifty/fifty." Peggy put her hand to her mouth, and tears filled her eyes.

"Oh my God," she whined. "Oh no, this can't be true."

"I'm sorry to say this, Peggy, but you haven't heard the worst. She suffered very severe burns on her face, neck, and body. She has sustained major multiple fractures to her face. Basically, her face was crushed completely, and it will be very challenging if not impossible to try to reconstruct it. She has also lost an eye, an ear, an arm, and a leg." Peggy looked at him in total shock, unable to speak.

"She is in a state of great shock and in a coma, and like I said, it's a miracle that she's still alive. We will know in the next few days if she will make it." He put his hand on Peggy's, who was sobbing uncontrollably by now.

"Oh my God, this is terrible, poor Linda, oh my God." Peggy was in a state of complete turmoil. Dr. Hall held her hand and waited in silence while Peggy absorbed what he had told her. It was not the first time in his long career that he had been the messenger of bad news to family or to friends.

"Can I see her, doctor?"

"Sure, but only for a few minutes. She's in a coma and heavily medicated and unable to communicate. Will you be calling her next of kin, Peggy?"

"Yes, I will. I'll go see her, and then I'll call her mom."

"Okay then, come with me." He rose and led the way.

An aseptic tent covered Linda's bed; everyone had to wear masks and scrubs to get inside. Most of her body and all of her neck and face were covered in gauze or bandages; Peggy saw the bandaged stumps of her amputated arm and leg, and she seemed to be hooked up everywhere. Medical personnel were constantly in and out to take care of something or another. Peggy could not control her tears.

"Oh Linda, I'm so sorry," she sobbed silently, her body shaking violently. After a while she regained her composure and whispered to the unconscious Linda, "Linda, its' Peggy. I just want you to know that we'll get you through this, okay? Just hang in there for me, Linda. Just hang in there please." She broke into tears again, and Dr. Hall put a hand on her shoulder.

"Okay, Peggy, let's go now," he said softly.

"Okay, doctor." Peggy was devastated as she turned and walked out of the ICU.

She went back to their apartment and sat down in the living room with the phone in her lap. She took a long, deep breath and dialed Linda's mother's number.

Linda's mother arrived the next day. Peggy picked her up at the bus stop, and they rushed to the hospital. Peggy had been checking in on Linda's condition by phone every four hours, but nothing had changed; she was still listed as critical but stable. Peggy was obsessed with Linda's survival and she could not envision any other outcome. The thought of losing Linda was just too much for her to bear.

Linda's mother had a violent reaction when she saw her daughter in the hospital bed.

"Oh my baby, my baby," she wailed, Peggy had to take her out to the corridor to calm her down. She took her gently by the shoulders, drew her to her, and gave her a long, comforting hug. Then, while holding her firmly by the shoulders and with her eyes looking intently into hers, she said, "Listen to me, Mrs. Staunton, you have to be strong, tough like Linda is right now, okay? She needs us to fight with her, do you understand?" Linda's mother was in a state of shock, and she was too choked up by her emotions to be able to speak. She nodded her head to signify that she understood as tears poured down her cheeks. Her pain was too much for Peggy to bear and she choked up too. When their tears subsided, they encouraged each other and went back in to see Linda, talking to her and holding her hand during the few minutes they were allowed to stay in the ICU. Then they went to the hospital cafeteria for coffee and for a very long and a very miserable cry.

Somehow Linda Staunton survived that accident. Why, by what miracle and by whose hand? No one could answer those questions, but she survived. She was a broken and mutilated human being, but nevertheless alive, and considering the misery and torment that would certainly become the rest of her life, maybe she would have been better off to die. But such was not her destiny; she hung on ferociously, with an uncommon determination to live and to not let go. Maybe it was her friend Peggy's constant attention and care during her coma, or maybe it was a desire to live so profoundly embedded in her being that it made her quasi indestructible; whatever the reason or reasons, survive she did. For three months and three weeks she was in a coma, one hundred and eleven days. Then, one day, just like that, she woke up. She was totally disoriented and did not know where she was or what she was doing there. She could only see out of one eye and could not feel parts of her body. Two nurses rushed to her bedside and leaned over her, smiling; Linda looked from one to the other with a panicked look in her eye.

"Miss Staunton, you're awake, that's fantastic," the older nurse, Beth, said, leaning over her. "Now listen," Beth spoke loud and slow, as to a child who needs to understand that the conversation is serious, "you have had a terrible accident, and you have been in a coma for over three months. Please don't try to move or speak. You are still very heavily medicated, and a lot of your injuries are not healed. The doctor who treated you will be in to see you shortly, okay? Just stay put and everything will be fine. We will do everything we can to keep you comfortable, okay?" Linda looked from one to the other, a look of complete confusion in her eye. Since there were tubes in her mouth she could not answer, but she moved her head very slightly to indicate that she had understood.

The head nurse called Peggy at work. It had been agreed that she would call Peggy if there were any changes in Linda's condition. Peggy had been in every day to see her since the accident, before and after her shift. She spent her time there talking to Linda as if she were awake and making sure that she was comfortable and didn't need anything. She brought flowers and pictures of Linda's favorite animals at the clinic and she would softly play some of her favorite music near her ear and sing along to the tunes. Peggy was a one-woman army of dedication and love, and she was convinced that Linda knew she was there and fighting with her. Linda's mother had had to leave after ten days once Linda had been stabilized. She had a job to go back to and the other children to take care of. Peggy had taken charge of things and kept her informed by phone a few times a week. It had been a depressing few months for Peggy. Every day she would pray for her friend to wake up, and although her injuries were mending well and her general condition was getting better, she desperately wanted her to wake up. Peggy picked up the phone.

"Hi, Peggy, it's Beth from the hospital."

"Oh hi, Beth, what's up?" Peggy was concerned; Beth had never called her at work before.

"She just woke up, Peggy. It happened ten minutes ago. She's confused but okay."

"Wow." Peggy's hand trembled slightly. "I'm coming right away." She hung up before Beth could say another word.

Peggy was overjoyed, but at the same time, she was worried about Linda, who was in for a major shock. She arrived at Linda's door at the same time as Dr. Hall.

"Hi, Peggy, so you heard already, eh?"

"Yes, Beth called me," Peggy was out of breath. She had literally run to the ICU. "I'm so happy she's finally awake, but God I'm nervous. You know, of her reaction and all. Have you been in there yet?" Peggy pointed to the door of the ICU unit.

"No, I just got here. Look, Peggy, before we go in there, just a little advice. Linda is a very mutilated person. Later when we take off the bandages and gauze that she has wrapped around her head and she sees that more than half of her face is burned, crushed, and scared beyond repair, well, she will be in a state of absolute shock. Also, as you know, she lost a lot of body parts, and that will be brutal to absorb too. So, what I'm going to do is to take it real slow with her, and I need you to do the same, okay?" Peggy nodded her approval. "Just remember that if there ever was a time when she needed your love and support, it's now. It will be the worst time of her life. Do you understand what I'm saying, Peggy?" He looked at her intently; Peggy took a deep breath, opened her eyes wide, and lifted her shoulders, as if to build up her courage.

"Yes, Dr. Hall, I understand and I'm ready."

"Good then, thank you for her." He pushed the door open and allowed Peggy to go in first.

The nurses had removed the tubes from Linda's mouth and had propped her up a little in the bed. Her face and head and the whole top part of her body were still wrapped in bandages or gauze. Peggy could see the look of confusion and terror in Linda's eye as she approached her bedside with Dr. Hall. Linda's voice was raspy and faint.

"Peggy, what's going on?" Peggy leaned toward her, smiling.

"Oh Linda, I'm so glad you're awake." She turned and pointed to Dr. Hall. "Linda, this is Dr. Hall. He saved your life, you know."

"Hi, Linda, how are you feeling?"

"Okay, I guess ..." Linda's speech was difficult and slurred, and she was gasping for air after every word. Her good eye was darting left and right as if she were searching for her bearings. Dr. Hall stepped in closer.

"Look, Linda, you've been in a coma for a long time, and your body and mind need to adjust." He spoke loud and with authority because he wanted to be sure that she understood. "The important thing right now is that you rest and regain some strength. Just stay calm and let us take care of you, okay?" Linda looked from him to Peggy and nodded that she understood. Her eye was filled with interrogations and alarm. She looked toward Peggy perplexed. Peggy picked up on the cue; she imitated Dr. Hall and spoke loudly.

"Look, Linda, you've been in a very bad accident. You were hit by a car as you were going to work. You've been in a coma for a long time, and we didn't know if you would make it, so ..." tears swelled up in Peggy's eyes, "so today is a miracle." Her eyes were now filled to the brim, and she choked on her words. "I'm so glad you're awake, Linda. Just do as the doctor says and rest, okay?" She had difficulty pronouncing the last words, and tears were running down her face. Linda looked at her intently with her one good eye, and she nodded that she understood. She lifted slightly her remaining bandaged arm in Peggy's direction, and Peggy gently took it. Linda squeezed her hand and smiled.

Dr. Hall put his arm on Peggy's shoulder,

"Let's go now, Peggy. You can come back later, okay?"

"Yes, okay," she said, sniffling.

"I'll come back later, Linda, after work, okay?" She let go of Linda's hand, and Linda nodded her head and closed her eye slightly. She was still heavily medicated, and it looked like she was about to fall asleep. Peggy and the doctor left the room silently. When they were in the corridor, Peggy turned toward him,

"I'm sorry about that in there, doctor. I just couldn't help it. It was too much after all this time to see her awake and able to understand. I've been praying for this for months."

"Its okay, Peggy, no need to explain, look, can you come by my office later? I would like to talk to you about how I'll break the news to Linda about her condition; it's going to be hard, you know."

"Yes, I know. I'll come by and see you after work, okay?"

"Fine, Peggy, and thanks for everything. You've been a wonderful friend for Linda, you know. She is very lucky to have a friend like you." Peggy blushed and stared at the floor.

"Thanks, doctor. It's nothing, really. She's my friend, and I love her, that's all." He put his hands on her shoulders, and she looked up.

"No, it's not Peggy, what you did is very selfless and important, believe me, I've seen a lot of things in these years at the hospital. So don't you ever forget it, okay?" He looked at her intently and smiled. She smiled too.

"Okay I won't, thank you. I'll see you later then?"

"Yeah, later," Peggy turned and walked slowly down the corridor, her heart heavy. She knew that the next few days would be the hardest of Linda's life and probably of hers too.

During the next few days, Linda gradually regained her strength, and Peggy spent as much time as she could in the room with her. Whenever Linda was awake, Peggy went over to her bedside and would take her hand and say encouraging things to her. She had agreed with Dr. Hall not to discuss Linda's condition with her, and he had told her that he would inform her when he thought she was strong enough to handle the news. He had asked Peggy to be present when that time came. Linda would always ask Peggy questions when she was awake, but Peggy would just tell her to rest and that Dr. Hall would answer all of her questions soon. On the third morning of her coming out of her coma, Linda had told Peggy that she felt a tingling in her leg, indicating the side of her body that did not have a leg anymore. Peggy had not responded but had felt very uncomfortable. She believed it was time Dr. Hall told Linda about her condition. She went to find him and told him about the leg incident before he came around for his morning rounds. He had agreed with her that it was time to talk to Linda.

"I'll talk to her this morning when I come around, okay?"

"Yeah okay, doctor." Peggy felt terrible as she waited in Linda's room for him to show up.

At about eleven he came into her room. He was alone and not accompanied by his usual string of interns and nurses. He walked up to Linda and said, "Hi, Linda, how are you today?"

"Okay," she answered. Her voice was still a bit hoarse. Peggy came up to stand beside him.

"Hi, Peggy, I was just about to tell Linda about her condition, and I'd like you to stay, if that's okay with Linda, of course." Linda nodded her head. Peggy took her hand, and Linda noticed that her eyes were dark and filled with tears. She stiffened, sensing in their demeanor that something was going on. Peggy gently stroked Linda's hand and kept her gaze on her. The doctor cleared his throat and slowly began to explain to Linda in minute detail in what shape she had been in when she had arrived at the hospital.

"To be honest with you, Linda, you were practically dead, and nobody thought you'd make it, but you did, and that's a good thing." He smiled at her and then went on to explain how her face had been crushed and how severely she had been burned to her chest, neck, and face. He spoke very slowly, explaining everything in detail. He was very professional, and Peggy felt that he actually made the bad parts sound okay.

"Now, there is some more difficult news that I have to give you in all of this. Linda, as you have probably guessed, you have unfortunately lost some body parts as a result of your accident." He then went on explain slowly and gently that she had lost an arm, a leg, an ear, and worst of all, an eye. Linda squeezed Peggy's hand hard.

"I'm sorry to have to tell you this, Linda, but this is where we are. Now, I know this is terrible and devastating news, Linda, and that it is a lot to digest, but believe me there is hope. I will discuss later with you all the options you have as far as reconstructive surgery and artificial limbs are concerned. We have some fine surgeons, and they do some pretty incredible work. I wish I had better news Linda, but this is the reality of your situation. On the bright side of things, you are conscious and alive, and that is phenomenal, believe me. We will put you back together, Linda, I promise you that. You will not be the same person that you were, but you will be able to function. It will be a long, difficult, painful, and frustrating process, but you will succeed, I'm sure of that. You are the strongest person I have ever met, and I just know it in my heart that you have it in you to do this."

Linda had not reacted while he spoke; she had just squeezed Peggy's hand a few times. When he was finished, she extended her bandaged and trembling hand toward him; he stepped closer and gently took her hand in his own.

"Thank you, doctor; thank you for saving my life," Linda said bravely with a look of determination in her eye. Her voice, although altered by her crushed face, was cracked and choked by emotion. Peggy shuffled her feet about nervously. She had been anxiously looking from Dr. Hall to Linda and felt terrible for her friend.

"You're welcome, Linda. I'll need you to be strong now, you know?"

"I'll be strong, doctor. I promise you that. I didn't get this far for nothing."

"That's the spirit, Linda. Thank you. Now you just rest up and regain your strength, and I'll come in later to see how you're doing, okay?"

"Okay." Linda's voice exuded fatigue; those thirty minutes with Dr. Hall had seemed interminable and had taken everything out of her. Peggy stayed for a long time after the doctor had gone. Neither of them spoke, and tears poured down Peggy's face. She just could not stop crying. Linda held her hand and squeezed it occasionally, looking at her intently with her one good eye, her gaze strong and steady and filled with all the love she felt for her; Peggy, her one and only true friend, the one who had been there for her in her time of need and who loved her unconditionally. Linda did not cry that day; she did not have it in her at that time. The tears and the pain and the rage would come later.

Linda spent the next year in the hospital. They fitted her with an artificial arm and leg, and the surgeons redid her ear and she had a pretty convincing artificial eye fitted in. She was, however, horrible to look at, scary even. Her hair was stringy and thin and had no luster. The structure of her face had been altered, and the bones on one side of her face had been crushed to pulp. Half of her face was caved in and drooped, and her mouth and lips were permanently crooked. No amount of reconstructive surgery could correct that. When she spoke, it was from the side of her mouth. The burn marks on her face and neck were so severe that it had been impossible to hide the scars, even for the best cosmetic surgeons. They had encouraged Linda by telling her about a face transplant, but they knew it was still an experimental surgery and that it would be years before Linda would be in any kind of shape to even envision that possibility, if ever. Linda's life was a flurry of reconstructive surgeries, medication, and loneliness, intense and profound loneliness. Of course there was Peggy and her mother, but Linda understood that she was now alone in the world. She was alone like she had never been before in her life, with a now radically different physical appearance, an appearance that would make her life extremely difficult and most certainly fill it with pain and heartache.

The only exercise she got during this time was when she would walk up and down the hospital corridors at night when there was no one around. Once she had taken such a walk and she had not covered herself, as it was four a.m. and she was sure the corridors would be empty. As she passed in front of a room, a young couple emerged from it and came face to face with her. The woman shrieked as if she had seen a ghost.

Linda would never forget the look of sheer horror on the woman's face. They quickly passed her by, and she clearly heard what they said as they walked briskly away.

"Did you see that? My God, that was terrible."

"Shhh, not so loud, she might hear you."

"How can she live like that? Poor girl, it must be unbearable. I'm going to have nightmares about this."

"Not so loud. I said." The young couple did not realize how deep their words had cut and how hurtful their exchange had been to Linda. Of course, they were young and had only expressed what they were thinking. They certainly had meant Linda no harm, but it had hurt her to the very depths of her being. Linda had seen how they had looked at her, like a freak, and how they had cringed at the sight of her. She understood that their reaction was involuntary and certainly not malicious, but it became crystal clear to her at that time that even partially revealed, she was visually repulsive and a horrible sight to see. From that moment on, she always wore sunglasses and scarves to cover her head and as much of her face and neck as she could. Linda understood clearly her predicament and how dramatically her life had changed for the worse.

Finally Linda was sent home. She would continue to be followed medically for quite a number of years, but she was strong enough to go home. Peggy had helped her get comfortable in their apartment. She took care of everything— she paid the bills, did the groceries and the cleaning, and kept abreast of Linda's many doctors' appointments and visits to the hospital or rehabilitation center. Peggy was the only thing that had not changed in Linda's life. She was her anchor, and she didn't care how she looked. To her she was Linda, and that was that. Things were different, however, between them. They did not laugh as much as they used to, and they never did anything together outside the apartment.

Going out for Linda was out of the question, the only exception being if it was absolutely necessary for medical reasons. When she did go out for these occasions, she would prepare herself a day ahead of time. It made her very nervous, and she always wore her sunglasses and a hat and a scarf to hide as much of her head, face, and neck as she could. She would go as quickly as possible into the waiting taxi, so as to spend as little time as possible in the proximity of people in the building or on the street. She was very conscious of her horrible appearance and wished to share it with as few people as possible. Going out for any social occasion was a non-subject, as were men. Peggy knew better than to bring up the subject of boyfriends, past or future. That would have been like twisting a knife in Linda's wounds. Linda thanked God every day for Peggy's presence at her side, faithful, unfailing Peggy. She was Linda's only real contact to the outside world, except for the doctors and medical professionals that she saw on a regular basis. Linda was completely dependent on her for just about everything. Of course, she had the Internet and a television, but Peggy was a real person who talked to her about life outside the apartment and real people living a real life. Peggy was the only person besides her mother who Linda felt comfortable enough to be with, up close and personal that is, and who could make her forget her situation, even if it was only for a few hours.

"Hey, it's me, I'm home." Peggy always shouted when she got home. It gave Linda time to cover herself. Linda was okay with Peggy seeing her face, but it embarrassed her, and Peggy knew that, so she would shout to make sure she didn't startle her.

"I'm here, Peggy," Linda shouted back from the living room. "How was your day?"

"Great, hectic, though. It's been really busy at the clinic lately." Linda heard Peggy's keys rattle when she threw them on the kitchen counter, and she walked into the living room. Linda was propped up on the sofa with pillows. The television was on, and books and magazines were strewn about. She wore her usual black jogging pants and a white turtleneck that covered her neck well. Her head was covered with a light blue scarf, and she had a pair of lightly tinted sunglasses on. As usual, all the blinds were closed and the lighting was subdued.

"Hey you, what's up?" Peggy dropped into the sofa beside her.

"Not much. I'm feeling stronger every day, though, and you know what? I'm actually getting used to walking with this thing," she pointed to her artificial leg. "I could be good for dancing soon, you know?"

"You'd better be. I'm counting on that to happen." Peggy smiled; both of them knew it was a lie.

"That lawyer called again. You know the insurance company guy?"

"The one with the funny name?"

"Yeah him, anyway, he says he wants to meet with me to discuss my claim. I've talked with him on the phone a lot of times, but now he insists upon meeting me in person. I can't do this alone, Peggy. I need you to be with me. Will you?" It was obvious by the tone of her voice that Linda was very anxious about the meeting and still very fragile.

"Hey, come on, Linda, of course I will. You know that. You don't even have to ask me. I'm here for you, and I'll be here for as long as it takes, okay?"

"Okay, Peggy, thanks."

"Well, any night this week would be good for me, or Saturday—yeah, Saturday would be better, Linda. Look, this is what we'll do. We'll have him come here and that is nonnegotiable, okay?" Peggy looked at her sternly, and Linda acquiesced by nodding her head. "Fine, so before he gets here, we will dim the lights, and you can wear your scarf and glasses, that way you'll be comfortable and everything will be okay. What do you say?"

"That's sounds fine, Peggy, thanks. You know this guy; he keeps throwing all this legal nonsense at me. All I want is to settle this thing and get on with what's left of my life. I don't feel like reliving this forever. He asks me so many questions it makes my head spin." Peggy took her hand.

"Look, Linda, I'll help you get through this, okay? Together we can handle this guy. Don't you even worry about it? After all, he's only a fast-talking insurance lawyer, right? He's no match for both of us, believe me." Peggy patted Linda's hand affectionately.

"Yeah, I guess you're right." Linda was still doubtful. "He makes it sound like what happened was my fault; he's out of his bloody mind."

"He's just doing his job, Linda. It's all part of his lousy, stinking job. That's probably what this guy does for a living; he scares vulnerable people like you into settling so as to save as much money as he can for his company. Now please stop worrying. I promise you, everything will work out, okay?" Peggy looked at her intently, her gaze emanating strength and resolve.

"Okay, Peggy, thanks. I don't know what I'd do without you. You're my life saver." Linda leaned her head and rested it on Peggy's shoulder. Peggy gently put her arm around her.

"Hey, that's what friends are for, right?" She stroked Linda's stringy hair, and Linda nodded her head in agreement.

"Jeff Peterson has been asking about you again." Linda sat up. She had not seen Jeff Peterson since that wonderful night before her accident when he had kissed her. It seemed so very long ago now. He had sent flowers and cards to the hospital and had visited her during her coma, but once she was awake, Linda had not allowed him to come and visit her. He always passed his messages through Peggy, and he often left messages on her voicemail. Linda had never responded except to ask Peggy to say thank you for her for the flowers he'd sent and the messages. She had also sent him a thank you note when she had gotten out of hospital. In the note she had asked him to remain away from her and that she would contact him when she was ready to see him. But Linda knew that she was better never to see him again.

"Really?" Linda had trouble hiding that she was annoyed.

"Yes, really, you know he always asks about you."

"Well, just tell him I'm getting along fine with my recovery, okay?"

"Yeah, okay, I will." Linda felt that Peggy didn't like her answer.

"Look, Peggy, you've got to understand, I'm not the girl he met and courted. I'm a deformed and mutilated freak. He'll run out of here scared to death." Linda's voice was filled with pain and anguish. It hurt Peggy to hear that because she knew Linda was right, but Peggy was a fighter and would have nothing of it.

"Now you listen to me, Linda Staunton: you're not a freak, okay? You're the same beautiful person you were before, only your exterior has changed. So please stop saying things like that. It's very hurtful and makes me mad as hell, so stop it, okay?" Peggy had raised her voice; her tone was firm and laden with authority. Linda sunk back into the sofa.

"I'm sorry, Peggy, it's just that sometimes I get so mad and frustrated because of what happened to me. It's so bloody unfair." She began to cry softly, and she took Peggy's hand and squeezed it. "I'm sorry, Peggy, I'm so sorry."

Peggy took Linda in her arms again. "Hey, it's okay. You're allowed to be mad. Just don't go there on me, please. I can't help you if you're not with me 100 percent, Linda. I need you to fight with me, do you understand?" Linda nodded with her head still leaning against Peggy's shoulder.

"Anyway, Jeff was just asking about you. I think his concern is sincere. He's just reaching out, so please, at least give him the benefit of the doubt." Linda sat upright and wiped the tears from her face.

"You're right, Peggy. It's just that I'm not ready to even think about things like that right now. You understand that, don't you?"

"Of course I understand. Let's just leave it at that for now, okay? I'll tell Jeff you're fine and that you say hello."

"Yeah, okay."

"Hey, what do you say I go fix us some dinner?" Peggy got up.

"Yeah, good idea, I'm starving. What are you making?"

"Chicken cacciatore with pasta."

"Sounds great, can I help?"

"You just stay where you are. I'll do fine, and anyway that kitchen is too small for two people." Peggy went into the kitchen to prepare dinner. Linda thought about Peggy, who was sacrificing so much to take care of her. "God I love her. She's such a true friend." She secretly feared the day that Peggy would meet a guy and fall in love. She couldn't imagine her life without Peggy in it.

While Peggy was busy in the kitchen, the phone rang. Linda saw it was her mother, and she picked up.

"Hi, Mom."

"Hi, sweetheart, how are you?"

"I'm getting better, stronger every day, and you?"

"Oh the usual, you know, work, the children. Everyone says hi, and Grandma Flo sends her love." Linda could hear them in the background.

"So do I, Mama. Tell them I send them my love, and I miss them all very much."

"We miss you too, Linda, and our thoughts and prayers are with you every day."

"I know, Mama, thank you for that. I really appreciate it." Linda talked a while with her mother, and then everyone else came on the line to say hi. They had been doing that a lot since Linda's accident. It was Linda's salvation to be able to talk to her family often; it helped her get better to know that they were out there and that they loved and supported her. The longest conversations were with her mother, though. She gave her news of the family and the hometown, and Linda would tell her about her medical situation or upcoming operations. Peggy showed up in the living room and indicated that dinner was ready.

"Mom, I've got to go now, dinner is ready. Are you still coming next week?"

"Of course, Linda, I wouldn't miss it for the world. You know your brother and sisters would love to come too. They're all very anxious to see you and to hug you."

"I know, Mom, but I'm not ready for that right now." There was a silence at the other end of the line for a few seconds.

"Sure, Linda, I understand. In due time, eh?"

"Yes, Mama, in due time, I love you, Mama."

"I love you too, sweetheart. Bye now." Linda hung up.

The girls had a nice, tranquil dinner. They enjoyed each other's company immensely. Peggy was a fountain of conversation and anecdotes, and she brought light into Linda's bleak existence at a time when she most desperately needed it.

That Saturday morning, at twenty minutes before eleven, the buzzer of the girls' apartment rang.

"Shit, that's him already," Peggy shrieked. She was sure it was the insurance company lawyer who had arrived early. The girls had not expected him before eleven. She got up from the breakfast table and scurried about, closing all the blinds, turning on a lamp in a corner of the living room, and rushing to her room to get dressed. Linda was slowly making her way back from the bathroom and walked with difficulty because of her artificial leg and the cane. She had heard the buzzer from the bathroom.

"Is that him already, Peggy?" Peggy came running out of her room while buttoning her blouse.

"Yeah, I think so. Come on, let's settle you in." She helped Linda into the living room. The buzzer rang again, this time more insistent. "Okay, okay I'm coming," Peggy shouted in the direction of the door. She helped Linda sit down and cover herself and put on her sunglasses.

"Who is it?" Peggy asked while looking through the peephole.

"It's Mortimer Roaden from the insurance company to see Miss Staunton." Peggy opened the door.

"Oh, hello, won't you come in, sir. I'm Peggy, Linda's roommate." Peggy shook his hand. "She's expecting you; may I take your coat?"

"Yes, thank you. I'm sorry I'm a bit early. I hope that I didn't catch you off guard?" That was a lie, of course; Mortimer Roaden always arrived early. He loved to come into people's lives when they were not quite ready. Sometimes he stumbled on things, or he learned something in those precious early minutes, something that he wasn't supposed to know or to find out and something that could reduce the claim for the company. After all, that was his job, to make sure that the company, in the case of Linda it was companies, paid out as little money as possible to anyone. As he often told his colleagues, "I work for an insurance company, not a charity organization," and he would chuckle at his own wittiness.

"No, not at all sir, and like I said, we were expecting you." Peggy looked him over. He was small in height and thin, nearly skinny. He had sunken cheeks and a much too big curly black mustache for his face. His two front teeth were large and protruded from his mouth and made him look like a rabbit. His suit, tie and used black briefcase were all from another era and would have been more befitting for a man of sixty-five, but certainly not for him, who could not have been a day older than thirty-five. When he walked, his head hung forward a bit, as if he had had an extension installed for his neck, and his shoulders were stooped like those of an old and tired man. His whole demeanor and his ridiculous name fit perfectly with the job he did. Peggy concluded, "I'm sure he was born exactly as he is today, wearing his suit and his mustache and working for an insurance company." Peggy felt like laughing, but she restrained herself.

"Please, Mr. Roaden, right this way. Linda is in the living room." Peggy showed him into the living room and sat him in a chair directly in front of Linda. She went to sit beside Linda on the sofa.

"I thought that if you sat there you would be able to take notes because of the lamp." Peggy pointed to the open lamp behind him.

"Yes, it is a bit dark in here, thank you," he said while rummaging through his briefcase that he had placed on his knees. "So, how are you, Miss Staunton?" he asked with his head buried in the briefcase. He retrieved a pair of glasses and a notepad and closed the briefcase, placing it on his knees and setting the notepad on top of it. He slowly put on his glasses and looked toward Linda for the first time. He could not make her out well in the semi-darkness of the room and was surprised by the setting and how she hid herself with her scarf and sunglasses. He remained stoic, however. After all, he had seen many unusual things in his career, and he was not going to let the ambience of the place make him stray from his game plan.

"I'm okay I guess, all things considered." Linda was wary of him. She had spoken to him often on the phone, and she knew that there was a pretty tough person hidden behind the insurance geek appearance. It was the first time she had ever seen him, though, and he was not at all like she had imagined. She had thought him to be much older.

"Would you like some tea or coffee, Mr. Roaden?" Peggy wanted to be useful and to do something nice. She believed that he couldn't be as bad as Linda had described him to be. He appeared to her to be inoffensive and manageable enough. Roaden jumped on the occasion to be alone with Linda, even if it was only for a few minutes.

"I'd love some tea, miss …" he hesitated.

"Peggy."

"Yes, Peggy, tea would be nice."

"Okay, tea it will be," Peggy looked toward Linda, who motioned that she didn't want anything, and Peggy left the room.

"So, Miss Staunton, like I said on the phone, I have a number of questions for you. Just a few odds and ends I need to clear up so that we can move things forward." He smiled his best rabbit teeth smile, but Linda remained of stone.

"Go ahead that's what you're here for, right?" Linda was not buying his "let's get friendly" routine. One thing she had figured out from her conversations with him was that he was not her friend. Roaden cleared his throat,

"Yes, of course." He pulled out a large Mt. Blanc from his jacket pocket; it was ridiculously large. He placed the cap on his briefcase and cleared his throat again. Linda felt like laughing when she saw the large pen in the hand of such a diminutive and unusual man. It was the first time that she had felt like laughing in a long time. Mortimer Roaden, she concluded, was the most ridiculous and amusing man she had ever seen.

"So, Miss Staunton, everything is okay on the medical side of things. I mean, things are progressing normally?"

"Yes, I'm feeling better. There are still some operations left, as you know, and then rehabilitation for quite a while—I guess, probably forever." Linda pressed on the last word, leaving it hanging in the air; she understood perfectly the effect the word would have on an insurance lawyer. Mortimer Roaden did not miss a beat.

"Good, I've been following your case since the beginning, as you know, and that's what the reports say, but it's always nice to hear it from the person involved." He looked in her direction, but in the semi darkness he could not see her very well and because of the sunglasses she wore, he could not judge the effect his words were having on her or not. He did not feel in control, and he did not like that. He was a bit intimidated, but he did not let it show, and he valiantly pressed on.

"Very expensive case for us Miss Staunton, as you can surely imagine. That is the reason I have to follow things so closely. I do hope you understand." Linda did not answer. His attempt to soften her up was not working. Peggy returned and served the tea. The next two hours were an in-depth question and answer session. Mortimer Roaden was thorough; he went over every detail of the accident, of every operation, and of every medical report. He took notes methodically and in silence. Then, he would go to the next question. Of course this was all part of his work strategy. "Wear them down a bit. It never hurts," he believed. He especially loved it when people became impatient, "As these two were getting," he surmised. "That's when they make mistakes and can say things that can compromise or diminish their claim." Mortimer loved this time. After all, he was in no hurry; he had nothing else to do and had no life of his own. Linda noticed that he was enjoying his little game, and she decided that she had had enough of it.

"Mr. Roaden, I have a question for you." He looked up from his note taking.

"Yes."

"You are a full-time employee of the insurance company, aren't you?"

"Yes, Miss Staunton, that's correct. I'm one of their full-time legal advisers. It will be ten years next year that I have been with the company," he added, beaming, obviously proud of that fact. "Why do you ask?" Linda did not answer but pressed on.

"Now your job is to evaluate and to settle claims, right?"

"Correct." He did not like the tone she was using with him, and he became tense.

"So, since you work for the company, your first loyalty is to them, right? I mean they pay your salary, they sign your paychecks, and you do not, therefore, work for me, isn't that so?"

"Yes, of course Miss Staunton, but we also have very much your interests at heart that I can assure you."

"I'm sure you do, Mr. Roaden, but if you could find a way to reduce or invalidate this claim in any way, you would do it, because that is your job, to save money for the company that hires you, isn't it?"

"Yes, but I guarantee you that my company would never do anything that is improper. We play by the rules, and we have enormous consideration for you, as we do for all of our clients. After all, we are responsible for you, and I assure you that my company will assume its responsibilities." He had become defensive.

"Answer my question, Mr. Roaden." Linda was terse and directive. Roaden balked.

"Well, yes, if I find something in the course of my investigations that justifies the re-evaluation of a claim, then it is my duty to advise my superiors of the situation." He was getting worried now; Linda had not hired a lawyer yet to represent her, and he desperately wanted to keep it that way. A lawyer would make the price of settling her claim a lot more expensive, which in turn would not be good for him. He tried to change the course of the conversation and to retake control.

"Look, I'm sorry for all the questions, but I have to do a complete investigation in a professional manner. It is my responsibility and my job, as I have to do in all my cases." Linda remained silent for a calculated moment, content that she had made him uncomfortable.

"Fine, Mr. Roaden. I'm sure that you are a true professional and a very loyal person. I just want you to understand that I know where you're coming from and whom you work for. Now if we have finished this little Q and A, I would like to rest. All this has made me very tired. " Linda was surprised at her own aplomb and the harsh edge in her voice.

"Yes, of course, Miss Staunton, I appreciate the effort you have made, and I know how difficult this is for you, and believe me I will do everything in my power to get this claim settled as soon as possible." He put his teacup down, shaken by her firmness and fearlessness of him. He cleared his throat one more time, making more noise than usual this time. "Unfortunately, Miss Staunton, I do, however, have a last question that I have to ask you. I want you to understand that this is a question that I have been asked to ask you and that I do not agree with the question, but it is my duty to ask." That was a lie, of course. It was his question, and as always, he kept his most difficult and intrusive questions for last; it was his tactic, to push a person to the limit. Although he was uncomfortable with the present situation, he decided to go for it anyway. He had not come here to be pushed around like this, and he wanted to test Linda Staunton's limit.

"Fine, Mr. Roaden, do ask."

"Well, let's see, this is rather difficult," he coughed. "We need to know at what time you think you'll be considering going back to work, Miss Staunton. I mean, we understand that with the leg maybe you'll need a job sitting down and that can be worked out, I'm sure. Maybe we can even help you with that ..." He stopped talking when he saw Linda trying to get up; she was having difficulty and leaning heavily on her cane. Slowly she made her way over to where he was sitting. He looked up at her, not knowing what to do or say. In the light of the lamp, he could make out that she was a sorry sight to see. She took off her sunglasses and scarf and leaned toward him, putting her deformed and scarred face as close to his as she could. She stayed there for what seemed like an interminable amount of time to him, staring him down intensely with her one good eye. He leaned back in his chair, speechless and horrified. Linda did not utter another word and turned around and wobbled out of the room in the direction of her bedroom, slamming the door shut with a loud bang.

Mortimer Roaden rose, flushed and shaken by what he had just seen. Although he had seen the pictures of Linda

Staunton after her accident, he had never in his professional life seen someone so mutilated that close. He quickly picked up his things.

"I didn't know it was that bad. My God, I'm sorry I asked that question. It's so insensitive of headquarters, how could they?" Peggy was in shock and said nothing; they stood facing each other for a few awkward moments.

"Well, I'll be off now; we will finish this some other time over the phone. Please tell Miss Staunton that I am profoundly sorry, very, very sorry." He actually sounded sincere.

"Okay, I will, Mr. Roaden. It's been terrible for her, you know, just terrible." The look of Linda's face flashed into Roaden's mind, and he shook his shoulders as a shudder passed through his body,

"Yes, terrible, the worst I have ever seen. Well, thank you, and good day now." With those words he was off, praying for two things. First that Linda Staunton would not lawyer up on him. He knew that if he made a good deal in this case, a good deal for the company, that is. This would help his career tremendously. God forbid that a jury should ever hear this case or see that face. It would turn out to be a very high multi-million dollar settlement in her favor for sure. He had to find a way to put it to bed quickly and efficiently, and if he brought it in below the mark the insurance companies had set, it would make him look good with his bosses, and it could mean a promotion for him. The second thing he prayed for was that he would never ever have to see that face up close again. It had been a horrific experience, and he would never forget it. When he got outside, he leaned against the building, clasped his briefcase to his body, and closed his eyes, breathing in the cool, crisp air. After a few moments he reopened his eyes and shook his head again, hoping to erase the vision of Linda Staunton's mutilated face from his mind. Then, he readjusted his tie and with his head extended forward and his shoulders drooping, he was quickly on his way, to tend to the other business matters of the day.

"Linda, Linda, he's gone." Peggy was at Linda's door. She raised her hand to knock again, and at the same time the door opened and Linda appeared.

"What an asshole. I'm really sorry he upset you. Are you okay?"

"Yeah, I'm okay." Linda put an arm on Peggy's shoulder, and with her cane in the other hand, she began to walk toward the living room. Peggy put her arm around Linda's waist and walked with her, hoping she hadn't been too hurt by Mortimer Roaden's insensitivity.

"Tell me, Peggy, do you think his ancestors were rabbits or guinea pigs?" Peggy turned toward Linda and realized that she was making a joke. She smiled,

"I'd say a short, skinny rabbit with a long neck and a big fat mustache"

"A mustache two times too big for his rabbit face and a pen much too big for his little rabbit paws," Linda added, and the two girls roared. They reached the living room still laughing and with their bodies shaking. The laughter released the tension they had accumulated before and during their meeting with Mortimer Roaden. The ridiculousness of his diminutive character had made the whole scene surreal and almost burlesque. The girls laughed to tears. It felt good to laugh like that again; neither of them could remember the last time they had done that. They laughed until their sides hurt and they could laugh no more.

Of course, what Mortimer Roaden did not know is that Linda Staunton in her long period of convalescence and recovery had thought very carefully on the matter of her insurance claims. She knew her condition was worth a lot of money, and she also knew that insurance companies had not gotten rich by being nice to people like her and paying out large amounts quickly. So, Linda had put on a bit of a show for Mortimer Roaden, and she now knew she was ready for anything he would throw at her. She felt she could take on all the Mortimer Roadens of the world. There was, however, one thing that Linda was not prepared to do or to go through with and that was a long and outdrawn lawsuit and the subsequent public trial that would ensue. So, against her mother's and Peggy's advice, she had decided not to hire a lawyer.

"Hell, I can't face a lawyer, not even my lawyer." Linda raised her voice every time the question was brought up by either one of them.

So things had stood ever since she had left the hospital. The insurance company had paid all medical bills and given Linda sustenance money pending a final settlement of her case. The first visit of Mortimer Roaden announced to Linda that settlement discussion time was near, and she decided it was time for her to get ready for their next encounter.

The next morning Peggy was sitting at the kitchen table reading the Sunday paper. An unfinished croissant sat in front of her, and she had a coffee in her hand. She looked up when she heard Linda shuffle in; Linda had her shawl and sunglasses on.

"Hi, how are you today?"

"Good, I'm fine, and you?" Linda sat down and leaned her cane on the table.

"I'm great. What would you like for breakfast?"

"A croissant and a coffee sound like a good idea."

"Okay, coming right up." Linda extended her artificial leg with her hand to make herself more comfortable.

"Peggy?"

"What?"

"I need to upgrade my computer and a good printer. Do you think you could handle that for me? I mean on the financial side, until I get my claim settled." Peggy paused a moment,

"Sure, Linda, if we don't go out and get the latest most expensive everything, I think I can manage it."

"No, I just need a better laptop that has all the latest programs and upgrades." It was the first time since she had left the hospital that Linda had showed any real interest for anything. Peggy was attentive and more than willing to get her what she wanted if it was to stimulate her in any positive way.

"I work nights this week, so I can take care of that tomorrow if you want, any computer in particular?"

"No, I'll trust your judgment on that and don't forget the printer."

"Okay, done. I'll take care of it first thing tomorrow."

"Thanks, Peggy, I really appreciate it."

"Yeah, sure, here, a croissant and a coffee," Peggy placed the items in front of Linda and sat back down. She picked up the newspaper again and resumed her reading.

"Aren't you going to ask me what for?" Peggy looked up.

"What?"

"You know the computer and the printer."

"Oh yeah sure, what for?"

"Well, I've been doing some research on personal injury cases like mine and I found a ton of information on the Internet. It has helped me understand my own situation, you know from a legal perspective. I need a faster computer and a printer to prepare myself for the settlement discussions."

"I see, but I still think you should get a lawyer."

"Peggy we've talked about this before please." Peggy raised her hands in a gesture of rendition.

"Hey, I'm just saying, okay?"

"Okay, you want to know what else, Peggy? I'm going to kick Mortimer Roaden's ass. That little weasel is in for a surprise, believe me."

"Well actually, he looks more like a deformed rabbit, remember?" Both girls broke out laughing as they had done the day before. It felt good to laugh again. It was like old times, the times before the accident, when they were young and carefree and had not a worry in the world. Both of them knew that time was over though and that their laughter was only a momentary passage, a small break that life was giving them, like the sun breaking through the clouds on a troubled day.

Linda's mother came to visit the next week, as she did every month. She was the only other person besides Peggy that Linda would have in the apartment living close to her. She always cooked and cleaned, which gave Peggy a welcome break. She gave Linda news about Derek and her sisters, Veronica and Dawn. They were all getting on with their lives. She would describe in great detail everything that was going on in each one of their lives. It helped Linda stay in touch with her brother and sisters without actually having to see them.

"Linda you can't spend six hours every day in front of that thing. It can't be good for you." Her mother was not of the computer generation and didn't really understand or trust them. She worried that it was not good for Linda to spend so much time at the computer because of her fragile state.

"Oh come on, Mom." Linda was glued to the screen. "You know I have to do this. I'm educating myself, and I'm getting ready. I've really got to do this, Mom."

"Well whatever, it still doesn't seem normal. I mean, you spend just about every waking hour in front of that damn thing."

"It's not a thing, Mom, it's a computer." Linda closed the computer down; slowly she got up and shuffled over to sit with her mother, who had been absentmindedly watching television in the living room.

"You know, Linda, I don't understand how people get hooked on these soaps. I just don't get it." Linda's mom had not had the luxury of becoming a daytime soap-opera addict. The only thing she had ever known was hard work.

"It's simple, Mom. They've got too much time on their hands, and these things," Linda pointed to the television set, "well; they just fill up the emptiness in their lives. They don't know what it's like to have it rough, Mom, and they aren't tough cookies like you." Her mother turned toward her.

"I'm not a tough cookie, Linda; I've had a tough life, that's all. Life has made me what I am," she turned off the television. "You're gonna have to be tough too now, Linda, tough as hell. I worry a lot about that, you know."

"I know you do, Mama, but I'm tough. Believe me, I am, and I'm a fighter. I don't abandon easy, just like you didn't abandon easy when you had to raise us all alone. You didn't run. You dug in, and you fought for us, and we all made it because of you. Don't worry about me, Mama, I'll be fine."

"It's hard not to worry, Linda. You're here," she looked about the apartment, "all alone, so far from all of us who love you and miss you."

"I know, Mama, I miss you all too, but I'm not alone here. I have Peggy, and you come to visit me often." Her mother did not respond. She had tried to coax Linda into moving back home with her, but Linda would have nothing of it. She was stubborn as hell, and her mother knew that she would have things her way no matter what.

"Mom?"

"Yes dear."

"Tell me about Dad; will you, about you and him? I want to know, Mom, I need to know. I know he hurt you bad and that you've never wanted to talk to us about him, but I really want to know, please?" Her mother looked at her resigned.

"What is there to say, Linda? We were young, we fell in love, and I got pregnant with you. We got married, and then the other children came along quickly. Life took over our lives; there was never any time or enough money for anything. Your father was not an educated man. He worked as a laborer. The wages were bad and the work was hard. At one point there was no more love in our lives. I don't know how or when it happened. It just happened, that's all. Everything was work, laundry, children, housework, cooking, and that was it. That was our life. Then one day, he didn't come back from work. I never saw or heard from him again. He just left me there, in poverty with four children from nine to four years old, to raise on my own. He killed me, that bastard; he killed me years before my death." She turned her head away, tears filling her eyes. The memory of her long-gone husband had reopened the deep and bitter wound it had inflicted on her. Linda put her scarred hand on her mother's forearm. Her mother wiped her tears with her other arm and turned toward Linda.

"The only thing that kept me going was my love for all of you. From that moment on everything I did was for your sake and for your sake alone. Your father is dead for me, Linda, and he's been dead a long time, and I hope that he suffers as much as I have in this life." Tears rolled down her cheeks, and she lowered her head.

After a few moments of silence, Linda said, "Thanks, Mama. You know this is the most you ever told me about him. I appreciate it, and I promise you I won't ask or pry again. I just needed to know and to hear it from you, that's all." They sat there in silence for a few minutes, each one reflecting on what had been said.

"Do you want some tea, Linda?" Her mother asked her voice cracked with emotion.

"I'd love some tea, Mama, thanks." Just as she was about to get up, Linda took her mother's forearm and pulled her toward her. She took her in her arms and hugged her, pressing her good arm into her mother's back. It was the first time since her accident that Linda had held someone in that way. She held onto her mother tightly, not wanting to let go, and then the tears came, timidly at first and then in an unstoppable flow, and she began howling and sobbing uncontrollably, her whole body shaking with all the pain and tears that had been pent up inside her since her accident. It was as if the flood gates of her immeasurable misery had suddenly been opened.

"I love you, Mama," she wailed. "I love you so much." Her mother did not answer but held on to her daughter tightly, crying in silence and rocking her gently like a baby. They stayed that way for a long time, consoling themselves in each other's arms and sharing the weight of Linda's stupendous pain.

Jeff Peterson kept leaving messages on Linda's voicemail; he even sent flowers once in a while. Linda felt bad about not responding. Finally, one morning, after having built up enough courage, she called the clinic. After what seemed an interminable amount of time, he came on the line.

"Hello, Jeff Peterson here."

Linda opened her mouth, but she could not bring herself to speak. The sound of his voice brought back the memory of that last night, that night when their burgeoning love had taken its flight. That wonderful night that had been the last night of her other life—it all seemed so far away now.

"Hello, is someone there?" There was a touch of impatience in his voice.

"Jeff?" Linda's voice was cracked and hesitant.

"Yes?"

"Jeff, its Linda, Linda Staunton." There was a second or two of silence on the line.

"Linda, oh my God, Linda! It's you, wow! I'm so glad you called." Linda's voice had changed a lot because of her facial deformities, and he barely recognized her.

"I'm sorry I didn't call you earlier, Jeff. I mean, you've been so sweet and all, the flowers, the messages, it's just that, well ..." Linda hesitated.

"Linda, it's okay. Peggy has kept me up to speed on things. I know all about your situation, so it's okay, you don't have to worry or explain. I understand."

"Thank you, Jeff. I appreciate your concern and support. It helped me get through this ordeal, and I just wanted to thank you personally."

"Well, it isn't much really, a minimum, I might say, considering what you've been through. I was really concerned about you for a while back there. Your condition was pretty scary, you know. Anyway, the important thing is that you're getting better and that you called. I'm really glad you did that."

"Thanks, Jeff. Look, I'm sure you're busy, and I don't want to take up too much of your time ..."

"Take up as much time as you want, Linda. I'm glad to talk to you. It's been a long time, you know?"

"Yeah, I know. Anyway, look, I know you've asked Peggy a lot of times and you said in your messages that you wanted to come over and visit me and all, but ..."

"Yes, I'd like that very much, Linda ..." Linda cut him off.

"Look Jeff, I can't do that, okay? I just can't." Her voice was higher pitched, revealing her stress. "I need you to understand this, it's important to me." He was taken aback by her tone and sudden forcefulness.

"Okay," he said hesitantly. Linda sensed his unease.

"Look, Jeff, I'm sorry. I don't mean to be rude, but this is not something I will change my mind about. However, I do have a suggestion to make if you're interested."

"Okay, what is it?" He had become cautious; her tone had stung him and put a damper on his enthusiasm.

"Well, how about we communicate by email? That would work for me."

"Sure, Linda, that's a great idea, I'll drop you an email later today, as soon as I get a minute. It's been crazy busy here lately."

"Yeah, I know, Peggy told me all about it. So look, I'll let you go now. You have things to attend to, and we'll talk by email, right? Oh, and once again, Jeff, thank you for your support; it means the world to me."

"You're welcome, Linda. I'm glad you called and to know that you're doing okay. So you take care now."

"I will thank you. Bye now."

"Bye, Linda."

Linda stayed a long time by the phone after having hung up, staring in front of her at nothing in particular. When she had been on the phone with Jeff, she had felt like her old self again for a few moments. It had felt good to feel that way again, even though she knew she would never be that person again. She knew there was no place in her new life for Jeff Peterson, or anybody else, as a matter of fact, and she firmly believed that that chapter of her life was over.

Linda spent most of her days in front of her computer. She had two regular correspondents. One was Jeff Peterson, who had a talent for writing that he probably didn't even suspect he had. She loved to read his emails. They were always witty and funny and full of surprises. They wrote to each other two or three times a day sometimes. She got excited every time one of his emails came in; it was often the high point of her day. Jeff never asked her to go visit, and she never offered. Then all of a sudden his emails became less frequent and then stopped altogether. Linda was disappointed but not surprised. It was only much later that she found out from Peggy that he had begun dating another woman and that they were planning to get married.

Her other email regular was the befuddling Mortimer Roaden. He emailed Linda continuously, convinced that he was handling things well and that he was in control. Linda, who had become very confident because of the newfound knowledge that she had acquired by her intensive research on the Internet, was asking him much more pertinent and to the point questions. He was not getting the better of her. Mortimer Roaden took her very seriously, and he replied to her every query with diligence and exactitude. He also remembered from his one and only face to face with her that she was not someone he wanted to screw around with. Thus, another year went by, and Linda regained her strength and acuity. Her life was spent in front of the computer or watching television. On rare occasions she ventured out late at night for walks and always with her head and face very well concealed. Peggy and her mother remained her sole real contacts with the rest of humanity.

One night Peggy got home unusually late. It had happened a few times in the past months, and Linda had thought nothing of it. Peggy had told her that she had been working late at the clinic.

"Hi, it's me." Linda heard the familiar clinging of her keys on the counter.

"Hi," Linda called from the living room. It was past 2:00 a.m. Peggy came into the living room and went to sit in front of Linda.

"Still up?" Peggy asked. Linda shut off the television.

"Yeah, I'm not really sleepy, and you? Been working overtime again?"

"No, I haven't, Linda," Peggy was looking at the floor, her hands clasped together in front of her. She looked toward Linda with a strange light in her eyes.

"Well you've been out then? Why are you looking at me with that funny look? Have you been drinking?"

"No, of course not," she said and smiled. "I've found someone, Linda," she said, her voice practically inaudible. "I've been seeing him for the past few months or so. I didn't want to tell you until I was sure it was serious." Linda just stared at her. It had crossed her mind a few times that Peggy would someday meet someone and fall in love. She had always pushed those thoughts out of her mind, secretly hoping that all that was a long way off. She now realized how selfish and stupid she had been and was in shock. She hadn't foreseen this happening so quickly.

Hiding her emotions, she asked in as casual a manner as she could muster, "Well, aren't you going to tell me about this guy?" She hoped her voice was not too shaky, which would have betrayed the turmoil in her gut. Peggy got up and went to sit beside her.

"Oh, Linda, he's fantastic. He's everything I ever wanted a man to be. He's kind, considerate, sensitive, and he loves me more than anything in the world." Peggy was so enthusiastic and her eyes were filled up with so much love that

Linda could only smile. She was happy for her, happy for her friend.

"Does Mr. Fantastic have a name?"

"Terrance, Terrance Holden. Oh Linda, I'm sure you'll love him too. He's a salesman who works for one of the big companies that sells supplies to the clinic. That's how I met him; he's been after me for months. I resisted at first. I thought he was just another, you know, fast-talking sales guy. But then, six months ago, I accepted to have a coffee with him after work. Well, one thing led to another and ..." Peggy sighed, looking toward Linda with her eyes full of light.

"So now you're in love with this Terrance, right?"

"Oh yes, Linda, I'm madly in love, and so is he. We've talked about marriage and children and all that ..." Peggy hesitated before going any further, looking from the floor and then back to Linda. Linda put her hand on Peggy's.

"Its okay, Peggy, you're allowed to be happy and to have a life. I mean to be honest with you, I thought this would have happened earlier," Linda lied admirably considering the formidable ache that had just entered her heart.

"Oh really, Linda, do you think so? I was so worried about telling you all this. I mean, I didn't know how."

"Look, Peggy, it's been two years since my accident. For two years now you've been taking care of me and brought me back to life. You dedicated yourself heart and soul to me, and for that, I will be eternally grateful to you and in your debt forever." Peggy began to protest.

"Hush now, hear me out, please. Because of you I am where I am today. You gave me the strength to overcome the insurmountable difficulties I was facing. I will be okay, Peggy, believe me. I can make it on my own, and I know that now. As for you, well, you are a young, beautiful, healthy woman. You deserve to be with someone, to have a family and to have a happy, fulfilling life. I want that for you, Peggy. I want that more than anything in the world. You got that?"

Peggy's eyes filled with tears. "Okay," she managed to say before throwing herself into Linda's arms, sobbing, her heart filled with both joy and relief. Linda patted her back and stroked her hair.

"Come now, let's not get carried away. This Terrance has not taken you away from me yet, right?" Peggy broke away from their embrace and looked at Linda with tear-filled eyes.

"No he hasn't, not yet." She wiped the tears from her face and managed a smile.

"So let's make the best of the time we have together, what do you say?"

"Okay, Linda, the best, I promise you, the very best." Peggy hugged her again and held onto her tight. Linda stroked her back and stared silently into space.

Linda did not sleep well that night. She tossed and turned and woke up frequently. Her bones hurt, like they hadn't hurt in a long time. Finally, after a long, silent cry, she managed to sleep a few hours.

The next morning Linda was up first. She set the table and prepared breakfast. Peggy shuffled into the kitchen at about ten. It was her day off; she looked at the set table with surprise.

"Hey, you made breakfast."

"Yes, I did. Sit down." Linda served her a coffee. On the table she had laid out some sliced fruit with some yogurt and French toast, Peggy's favorite breakfast.

"French toast, great, I'm starving." Peggy was particularly well rested. Her confession to Linda the night before about Terrance had liberated her, and she felt great, almost buoyant. Linda sat down and noticed how happy Peggy seemed to be; it made all the pain and torture of her sleepless night go away. She wanted Peggy to be happy, as happy as she would never be.

"I have some news for you too, Peggy," Peggy, with her mouth full of French toast, looked up and nodded, with a questioning expression in her eyes.

"Well, our friend Mr. Roaden has made me a counter offer to settle my claim, and I think that I will accept it."

"Oh yeah, what's the offer now?"

"Twenty-one million," Linda said nonchalantly.

"Twenty-one million! Wow, that's a lot of money." Peggy practically choked and her eyes became round with amazement. "That's a lot more than the last offer, isn't it?"

"Yes it is, but you see, I've been twisting his evil little arm quite a bit, and he's really scared I will go to a lawyer. So, he has made me an offer to settle all claims, and I think I'll take it. It's more money than I'll ever need. I could give some to my mother and then get my life organized, you know? Move on." Peggy put her fork down, reflecting,

"I think that's a great offer, Linda. I mean seeing you don't want to go through with the whole court thing, and like you say, it's enough money. You could travel or do just about anything you want to." Peggy tried to sound optimistic, knowing that Linda's options were limited.

"Yeah, I think so too. The papers will be ready next week; I'll have to go down there, you know, to his office. Would you mind coming with me, Peggy? I'd hate to go there alone; I mean, I haven't been out in broad daylight among people in over two years except to go to the hospital in a cab, but that's different."

"Of course I'll go, Linda. I will be your witness sort of, but tell me, what about those papers? Shouldn't you have a lawyer look at them? I mean, you can't really trust a man like Mortimer Roaden?"

"I've done all that already, Peggy; I've had the documents reviewed by an attorney I found on the web. He's an independent expert in the field, and he has certified to me that all the documents are in order and ready to be signed by me. To be honest with you, Peggy, I'm anxious to get all this behind me."

"Yeah, I understand. Hey, Linda, you'll be rich," Peggy lifted her coffee cup,

"Here's to being rich." Linda raised her cup too. They touched cups and both said it at the same time, "To being rich!" Linda smiled. She was happy that the news of her forthcoming riches made Peggy happy, but she felt no joy at all. She would have gladly traded in all that money just to be her old self again.

The following week the girls got into a cab and headed to the offices of Mortimer Roaden. It was a harrowing experience for Linda, and she was very nervous about going to an office building filled with people. She had been nowhere in the past two years except to hospitals or medical appointments of one kind or another. But this was different, and she had butterflies in her stomach. Peggy had bought her a nice black felt hat with a veil that fell all around it. It hid her face well, and also she wore gloves and a scarf wrapped around her neck. Peggy had also shopped for her an elegant black two-piece suit and a nice pair of shoes. Her deformities were undetectable except for the cane and her awkward gait. Even with all these precautions, Linda was nervous and fragile.

The elevator on the way up to Roaden's office was full of people. Linda felt very uncomfortable. Her hand was sweaty inside her glove, but much to her relief, nobody paid any attention to them. They all seemed completely preoccupied with their own thoughts and unaware of the people around them. Linda reflected on the times when, like these people, she had ridden on an elevator or a bus and was in a hurry to get to where she was going and had taken no notice of the other people around her and had been oblivious as to who they were and to where they were going. She wondered about these people now, only inches away, in this crowded elevator, people who were so busy with their lives that they forgot where they were and who was is in their immediate surroundings. Her condition now made her acutely aware of all this. She felt the elbow of the man standing beside her brush against her forearm, and the contact sent a shiver of discomfort down her spine.

Mortimer Roaden was waiting for them at the reception; he had not changed a bit since their first and only physical encounter over a year ago. The suit was different, though, a bit crispier and probably new, and he was even more stooped forward than before. He greeted them with his rabbit teeth forward and his neck well extended.

"Miss Staunton, Miss Bale, how good to see you." He shook both their hands, Peggy's vigorously and Linda's a lot less. "Won't you come this way please?" He led them down the corridors and to the doors of a conference room. Linda was aware that people looked at them when they passed the reception area and as they walked down the corridors, but she did not feel bad about their looks. They just looked, that's all, no reaction. If they found this woman veiled, in black from head to foot and who walked with a cane odd, they did not let it show. It made Linda feel good and gave her a bit of much needed self-confidence. They entered the conference room; it was a very large room with a very long table that could probably sit twenty-five to thirty people. Two of the walls were completely covered in wall-to-ceiling windows. Two men were sitting at the far end of the table. They rose when Mortimer Roaden entered with them. One was tall and thin, and he wore a gray suit and had an innate coldness about him. The other was overweight, and his suit seemed to be choking him. His face was red, as if he had just exerted himself. Mortimer introduced them. They were also lawyers, and they represented the other two insurance companies that were involved in her claim. Everyone said hello and then sat down, except for Mortimer Roaden, who looked around nervously. This was his show, and he was tense and wound up like an old alarm clock.

"So, ladies and gentlemen, would anyone like anything?" He looked from side to side, "coffee, tea, water?" Linda answered for both her and Peggy from underneath her veil.

"No thank you. Please let's get on with this, Mr. Roaden." The other two lawyers signaled with their hands that they wanted nothing.

"Yes, of course, Miss Staunton, of course." He sat down between the two men, and Peggy and Linda were sitting to one side of them. Linda sank back in her chair hoping that the distance would make it harder for them to see her. The men did not look her way at all. They were not interested. After all, they had seen the photos from the hospital files, and they had read the reports. Everyone had documents in front of them that Mortimer Roaden had prepared for the meeting. Roaden cleared his throat.

"Very well, then, we all know why we are here, so I will read these documents out loud now." He looked toward the girls. "If you have any questions as I read, please feel free to interrupt me at anytime."

Peggy responded politely, "Thank you, Mr. Roaden."

For the next twenty minutes or so Mortimer Roaden read the settlement papers out loud. The only other noise besides his monotone voice was the shuffling of paper when everyone changed pages. When he was finished, he looked up.

"Now, Miss Staunton, I also have a signed affidavit from your lawyer, your expert, as you like to say. After all, you are, in a sense, your own lawyer." He smiled to Linda. "Anyway," he held up a document, "it is in the document booklet, last page and in this affidavit he confirms that these documents conform to all our agreements with you and that they are in good order and ready for you to sign them." Everyone shuffled the pages again, looking for the affidavit and reading it.

"Thank you, Mr. Roaden, I know. I spoke to him yesterday, and he explained it to me." Linda's voice was hoarse, and she wished she had asked for a glass of water.

"Now, does anyone have any questions?" He looked toward both the girls and then to the men on each side of him. They both signaled no.

"No, Mr. Roaden, I have no questions. All is as we agreed." Linda's voice was a little better and even emanated a certain amount of assurance even though for some reason an inner turmoil was agitating her and making her feel queasy and uncertain. It was not the settlement. She knew everything was good and the lawyer she had found on the Internet and who had acted as expert counsel for her had very carefully verified everything. It was something else—maybe it was the way the other two lawyers never looked her way and only looked toward Roaden or the documents, taking only fleeting glances in hers, or in Peggy's, direction. Maybe Roaden had told them about his experience with her and they were scared that she would repeat it. Whatever it was, she was anxious for everything to be over and to get out of there.

"Fine, Miss Staunton, then we can all start signing." He began signing the documents in front of him, and everyone did the same. When he was done, he passed his documents to the right and took the ones that the lawyer to the left of him had passed on to him. Soon all was done; Mortimer Roaden looked in Linda's direction and smiled.

"Oh, I almost forgot Miss Staunton, there is also this." He rose and pushed an envelope toward Linda. "A very nice check, I might add, Miss Staunton." He smiled his best rabbit teeth smile. Linda didn't answer, and she got up with the help of the table, picked up her cane, and put the envelope in her purse without verifying it. She stood there immobile, looking at the three men for a second or two, as if daring them to say something. Mortimer Roaden was still standing, with a smile frozen on his face. Finally, Linda broke the silence, "Good day, Mr. Roaden, it's been a pleasure doing business with you." She ignored the other two and turned and began to walk toward the door.

"The pleasure has been mine, Miss Staunton," Roaden said, still standing. "May I show you to the elevator?"

"Don't bother, I know the way out," Linda said, still walking away with her back to all of them. "Come on, Peggy, we're done here." Peggy stood up and smiled to the three men; she picked up Linda's documents and quickly followed in her direction. Once the girls had left the room, the men shook each other's hands, obviously very happy. One of the men, the large and sweaty one, turned toward Mortimer Roaden and said, "Well done, Mortimer. You've done it, congratulations; this claim could have cost us three or four times that amount if it had gone to court. Good job."

"Yeah, good job, Mortimer," the tall, silent one acquiesced.

"Thank you, gentlemen," Mortimer Roaden was beaming, content with the outcome and basking in his professional success.

In the taxi on the way home, Linda sat silently staring out the window. It was good to be out again, even though she was terrified of being around people and of their reaction to her. She enjoyed seeing people scurrying about their business and to be so close to the sights and sounds of the city. It made her feel alive and breathed energy into her. She realized how much she had missed it all, the trepidation and excitement of life. Only one thing made the day a bit somber for her and that was the thought that Peggy would be leaving her soon. It haunted her, and the same question kept creeping into her mind, "What am I going to do now? What am I going to do now?"

Events went into fast-forward from that moment on. Peggy and Terrance had decided that they would get married that summer, and as a wedding present, Linda had offered them a new house. The lease to the girls' apartment would also end that summer, and Linda wasn't going to renew it. All the furniture would be donated to charities. Linda had decided that she needed a change of scenery, to be somewhere else and to breathe some new air. She concocted a plan to travel the country and organized everything with the help of her best friend, the Internet.

Her mother visited regularly, and every time she came, she tried to convince Linda to come back home, but Linda would have none of it.

"No Mama, I won't go back home and that's that. I wish you'd stop insisting. It's not my plan right now, okay?"

"But what is your plan, Linda? Peggy is getting married next month, and you're leaving your apartment. What are you going to do? Where are you going to go?"

"Mom, like I told you before, my intention is to travel, okay? I have it all organized, and I know what I'm doing. Look, Mom, I need to get out of here and out there, into the world, okay?" Linda pointed toward the window. "Do you understand what I'm saying, Mom? I've got to get out there and learn to live as I am, with other people. I'm a different person now, Mom, not inside, of course, but the outer me, the one that is visible to others. I've got to find that person and to be able to do that, I have to be out in the world. Do you understand that, Mom?"

"Yes, Linda, I understand, but I'm worried about you and scared too. I mean, you can't just go out there and pretend …" she stopped in mid-sentence and looked up to Linda as if searching for words.

"What mom? What? Pretend that I'm not this deformed, crippled monster? Is that what you wanted to say?" Linda had raised her voice.

"No, of course not," her mother protested, but Linda was annoyed.

"Well, that's what I am, Mom, and I know it, believe me I do. I can see it and feel it every day, every night, every hour, and every bloody minute, okay?"

"Calm down, Linda, and please don't shout like that. I'm just worried about you, that's all." She began to cry softly.

"I'm not shouting, okay? I'm not shouting." Linda's voice was still slightly high pitched. She shuffled over to where her mother was sitting and put her arm around her and kissed her hair.

"I'm sorry, Mom, I'm sorry. I have no right to raise my voice like that, especially not to you, of all the people. Look, Mom, just trust me, okay? I'll be traveling in my own limo, and I'll stay in the best hotels. Everything will be fine. I'll call you regularly, you know I will, and if I need you, I won't be afraid to ask, I promise." Her mother nodded that she understood through her diminishing sobs. "I might stay a week here a month there, I don't know, but I'll be fine. Believe me, I'll be fine. I've got everything covered, Mom, even on the medical side of things. I'll be in touch with my doctors regularly and it'll be like I was still here. I'll be okay, Mom, just trust me, please?" Linda was whispering now and practically pleading. Her mother did not answer; she knew that this was a discussion that she could not win. Linda was a strong-headed person, and she would have things her way, no matter what.

So, Linda put her plan in motion. She had set her departure date for one week after Peggy's wedding. Since plane travel was unimaginable for her in her condition, she had decided she would buy a limo, but first she had to hire a limo driver, someone who would work full time for her and someone with credentials and class. After all, that person would be spending a lot of time with her up close and personal, and she knew that she had to choose right. She found one through the services of an exclusive placement agency that she had found on the Internet. He had an impeccable resume and was highly recommended. Linda did not meet him physically right away, but she interviewed him by phone and communicated with him by email. She had very carefully and very thoroughly explained to him what had happened to her and her physical appearance and condition. His name was Charles, and he was forty-seven years old. For the past fourteen years he had been the driver of a very wealthy southern woman who had passed away six months earlier. Charles was British and had been living and working in America for the past twenty-two years. Linda agreed to pay him a very generous salary and asked him to help her shop for a car that would be comfortable and well suited for long distances and her particular physical condition. Since she would need him for the day of Peggy's wedding, she had decided that that would be the day she would meet him in person for the first time.

Linda had shopped for everything she needed for the wedding on the Internet. "Thank God for the Internet," she constantly reminded herself. "How easy it has made my life." By the time her mother arrived three days before the wedding, all was set; Linda was ready for the wedding and for her imminent departure.

It was a beautiful wedding filled with all the ingredients that make such occasions a success. The magnificent June day was illuminated by a brilliant sun, and the sky was completely blue, without a cloud in sight. Peggy was excited and bubbly like freshly uncorked champagne. Her whole family was there, even some distant cousins she had not seen in years. Her pleasure was only equaled by her unconditional love for Terrance. Peggy was that kind of person, whole and completely invested in her relationships, be it man or woman; she did not know how to love any other way.

Linda had bought a very elegant lavender outfit with a matching hat and veil; she wore white gloves, and her neck was wrapped in a delicate light blue silk scarf. One had to look carefully to see any signs of her physical devastation. She had also bought an expensive new cane with a beautiful sculptured handle.

"Oh, Linda, you look fantastic," Peggy had exclaimed, Linda had just walked up the steps of the church, and Peggy was standing with her father getting ready to go inside. Charles was right behind her, and he was the reason she was late. Linda had just met him for the first time in person at her apartment. It had been an awkward meeting, as Linda was nervous, and he was very reserved. He was a tall, elegant black man with light brown skin and his eyes emanated sensitivity and strength and Linda immediately took to him. His voice was grave, and he had a charming British accent which she found adorable. Linda was already dressed for the wedding when he arrived, she served him tea and they drank it while measuring each other out. Charles was a listener and attentive to detail. He said very little about himself and questioned her at length about what she expected of him and how he could be of assistance to make her life as comfortable as possible. Linda liked him immediately; he was polite, perceptive, and discreet. Time flew by, and she did not realize how late it was. The ride to the church proved that Charles was also an excellent driver.

"I'm sorry, Peggy, I didn't see the time pass, but I guess I haven't missed anything yet. Oh, you look so beautiful in white like that, my God." Linda took one of Peggy's hands; the girls looked at each other for a few seconds, and a powerful surge of emotions passed through them.

"Hurry, Linda, go to your places." Peggy let go of her hand and motioned to her and Charles to pass by. Linda's mother was there with her two sisters, and Linda took her place beside her mother. It was the first time her sisters had seen her in over two years, and they were obviously nervous. The music for the wedding began just as Linda sat down, and Charles retreated to the back of the church.

"Hi, Mom, hi, Veronica, Dawn," Linda whispered as Peggy came down the aisle.

"Hi, Linda, we're so glad to see you," Veronica whispered back. She squeezed Linda's gloved hand and Linda squeezed back.

The ceremony was grandiose and solemn, and the church was filled to capacity with the families and friends of the bride and the groom. Linda couldn't help thinking throughout the ceremony that although she had only just turned twenty-five and was single, she would never experience what Peggy was experiencing at that moment. It was a realization that made her profoundly sad.

"Oh, Linda, come, let's go sit down over there." Her sister Veronica was motioning to a table at the reception hall following the wedding. Linda sat with her sisters for a long time; it felt good to be with them again. She hadn't realized how much she had missed them.

"I love college life Linda and plus Jack goes to the same school, you know." Jack was her boyfriend, and they were planning to get married after they graduated.

"Good for you, Veronica. I'm really proud of you, you know, and so is Mom." Linda couldn't help but think about the time not so long ago that she had gone off to school, full of hope and love for Richard. It all seemed so far away now.

"It would be nice if you came for Christmas this year, Linda," her younger sister, Dawn, suggested. "I mean, we could all be together again, like old times, you know." Dawn was two years younger than Veronica, and she worked full-time as a personal assistant. She could have quit her job and put herself through college, as Linda had given each one of them five hundred thousand dollars. But she kept her job because she said she liked it, but mostly because she couldn't bear the thought of leaving Keifer, her boyfriend, to go off to college.

"Keifer would love to meet you, Linda," Dawn insisted. "It would be great. Promise me you'll think about it."

"I will, Dawn, I promise, okay? And I'd love to meet Kiefer too." As the day passed, Linda felt more and more at ease with her sisters, and it felt good being around them.

Soon it was time to see the newlyweds off. They were leaving for their honeymoon, and everyone was kissing them and wishing them the best. Linda went up to Peggy and hugged her.

"Good-bye Peggy, my Peggy. Have a wonderful honeymoon. I'm going to miss you, you know."

"Me too, Linda, I'll miss you too," Linda's head was rested on Peggy's shoulder; she drew back, holding Peggy by the waist and looking at her intently. So much had passed between them, and now they were going their separate ways. If Peggy could have seen Linda's face behind her veil, she would have seen the tears that rolled down her cheeks.

"Oh, I almost forgot." Linda reached into her purse and pulled out an envelope and handed it to Peggy.

"This is for you, Peggy, for you and Terrance, of course." Terrance was looking at them smiling.

"But Linda," Peggy began to protest; Linda forced the envelope into her hand and closed Peggy's hand on it.

"Look, Peggy, you deserve everything that is happening to you, okay? Just be happy, please. Do it for me, will you? You're my best friend, Peggy, and I love you and I'm really happy for you." Linda let go of Peggy's hand.

"I love you too, Linda, and I'll always be there for you, no matter what. You can count on that."

"I know, Peggy, I know." The girls hugged again, and then Terrance took Peggy's hand and pulled her away toward the waiting limo. Confetti and cheers filled the air as the newlyweds drove away. It was only later that night when they had arrived at their hotel that Peggy opened Linda's envelope. Inside the best wishes card was a check for half a million dollars" Peggy stared at the check in disbelief and had a long, hard cry.

"Shall we be going, miss?" Charles had been close by all the time.

"Yes, Charles. I will say good-bye to my family, and then we will go."

"Fine, miss." He followed a few steps behind her as Linda went off to say good-bye to her mother and sisters. Her family was booked at a hotel near the airport; they were flying early the next morning, and it had been decided that they would say their good-byes after the wedding.

Her sisters got all choked up and cried, and Linda hugged them and assured them that she would be fine and that she would keep in touch.

"You make sure you phone me, Linda. I want to know how you're doing, okay?" Her mother couldn't help being overprotective.

"Yes, Mom, I'll call you often, I promise, okay?" Linda took her mother in her arms and gave her a warm hug. Slowly her mother disengaged herself from her arms and asked,

"So, Linda, when are you leaving, and if I may ask, where you are going first?"

"I'm leaving in a week Mom and I'm heading south." Her mother looked at her perplexed, but she knew better than to ask for more details. Had she done so, none would have been forthcoming.

Chapter 3

WANDERINGS

So began a new chapter of Linda Staunton's young life. The following week was spent cleaning out her apartment. All that she kept fit into four pieces of luggage. It was a wonderful summer morning when Charles came to pick her up; the apartment was empty except for her suitcases and some boxes that would be picked up later that day by a local charity.

"Good morning, miss, how are you today?"

"Good morning, Charles. I'm fine, thank you, and you?"

"Couldn't be better, thank you, shall I load the luggage?"

"Yes, please, thank you." Charles picked up some suitcases and headed toward the car outside. Linda stood for a few moments in the empty apartment, looking about; nearly three years had gone by since she had moved in with Peggy. It seemed all so long ago now. Many memories, good and bad, would be left behind forever. They had been years that had altered her life forever. The very integrity of her being had been fractured by fate, and she should by all accounts have been dead. Yet, here she was, mutilated but still standing and deformed but still alive. Buried deep within her heart and soul she felt strong, stronger than she had ever felt before in her life. Her whole being was possessed by an uncommon desire to live and to fight for her morsel of happiness. Linda knew it would be a tough fight and that many challenges lay ahead of her, but she was ready and was inspired by the certitude that she alone could save herself. She took one last glance around the room and walked out.

Linda sank into the luxurious upholstering of the back seat of the limo; the car was perfect and was exactly what she needed. Charles had organized it well. There was a small television and a sound system and a table that Linda could pull out and set up her laptop on. There even was a small fridge tucked into a corner. She took a deep breath beneath her veil. She felt liberated, and a current of nervous trepidation ran through her body.

Charles turned around toward her.

"So, where to, miss?" She had not told him where they were heading.

"South, Charles, let's go south, shall we?" Linda's voice was filled with anticipation. He smiled at her.

"Okay, miss, south it shall be," he turned around and set the car in motion. They were on their way.

Linda loved the road, and although she felt the presence of people all around her on the roads or at the road stops, she felt protected inside her limo, her intimacy intact. Within a few days, Charles and Linda had developed a routine. He would tell her where they would be at about six the next evening, and Linda would find a hotel or motel on the Internet that was near where they were heading. Charles always went to get the food or pay for the gas at the road stops; Linda would eat in the car, and if she needed to use the washroom, Charles would fetch the key and then drive her as close as possible to the door. He took care of everything and was extremely meticulous to preserve her privacy and make sure that she was comfortable at all times. At night Linda would eat alone in her room, or if there was no room service, at the nearest restaurant. Charles would always prepare her arrival in any dining area, making sure she had a table in a corner by herself and as far away as possible from prying eyes. He would also always brief the waiter or waitress who would be serving Linda, asking him or her not to stare and to act normal with her. When he felt that everything was ready, he would go and get her and accompany her to her table. Linda would always bring along a book or a magazine to read while she ate. Linda had offered many times to Charles to eat with her, but he had declined, insisting that his professional role of conduct did not permit him to do that. She was his boss, and he was at her service. He believed that it was inappropriate for him to eat with her, especially in public. Linda had been amused by that, but she had said that she understood and respected his professionalism. Charles was never far off while she ate, and he could be quickly by her side should she need anything. When she was done, he would accompany her back to her room. Linda was impressed with him. He had learned very quickly the kind of attention and support she needed, and he gave it to her, sometimes before she even knew she needed it. She thought he was simply amazing and couldn't believe the luck she had had in finding him. Every new day his impeccable consistency and thoroughness confirmed to her that he was truly a God send.

"So, Miss Linda, tell me, do we have a destination this morning?" Charles's question was part of their morning ritual before they hit the road.

"Yes, as a matter of fact, Charles, we do."

"Would you mind sharing that information with me, miss? Not that I need to know. We could always just go wherever the car takes us."

"No, I don't mind sharing at all, Charles, and I promise you this—I'll tell you as soon as I know, okay?" Charles broke out laughing; he had a rich, healthy laugh.

"Okay, miss, fine, you do that now. You know you have a keen sense of humor, miss."

"Thank you, Charles, and so do you." Linda looked up from her computer and stared out the car window. "Just drive toward the Interstate, will you, Charles? I'll tell you which direction we'll take when we get there."

"Okay, then, we're on our way."

So went the extraordinary voyage of the most unlikely pair of individuals that had ever hit the road. Anywhere they stopped on the road they attracted glances and stares. The car itself was a curiosity. It was long, black, and foreign, but it was the curtains installed all around the back windows that really attracted attention. Charles had put them in so that Linda could isolate herself from the sun or from prying eyes. When they were all closed, she could take a nap if she so desired. Anytime the black limo pulled up off the highway with the curtains drawn, it raised eyebrows and piqued people's imaginations. Then, when Charles got out of the car, tall, impeccably dressed in suit and tie, and with his chauffeur's cap on; well, that was simply the clincher. People would openly gawk at him and speculate wildly amongst themselves about who was in the car. Charles's phlegmatic demeanor and British accent added to the mystique and the mystery. Linda was amused by the effect they had on people. She was glad to be a part of something that fueled their conversations and their imaginations.

At first they went south, then west, crisscrossing the country at a nice, slow pace; after all, Linda was not in a hurry, and she had no set schedule or plan. Her tolerance to the travails of the road was about a month, so their pattern was pretty much built around that. They would travel the countryside for three or four weeks, and then they would stop in a large city for one, two, or three months. During the longer stays Linda would sometimes have some reconstructive work done on her mouth and face. Then it was back on the road again. In the cities they would always stay in the most expensive and comfortable hotels. For years this was their *modus vivendi* and their game plan.

Their routine in the cities was well regulated. Charles would check in with Linda every morning at nine to see if she needed him for anything. Sometimes she had him run some small errands for her, but most of the time he was off for the day. At the end of the day, he would check in with her again at six.

Linda stayed in her suite a lot and read and watched television. Every day she would go out for a walk, always with her scarf, hat, veil, and gloves. It was during those walks over the years that Linda had noticed that the only people who paid no or little attention to her were the homeless and the vagrants and the people who lived on the street. They were the only ones in every city she had been in who did not look at her as an oddity or a freak. This made her curious about them, and one day she decided to explore their world and find out more about them. So, she visited the parks and streets where they hung out and spent a lot of time observing them. She talked to all the ones who approached her for money or for cigarettes and had come to the conclusion that the best way to know more about them was to become one of them. So, she developed a routine to do just that.

Her routine was simple. Once Charles had checked in on her and was gone for the day, she would get dressed and get ready to go out. When she was ready, she would take her cane and a used leather bag and leave her suite at a brisk pace. She could walk quite fast with her cane now, and her eye was well adjusted to the veil, and she had practically no more fears about going out in public. The hotel lobby was busy, as all hotel lobbies will be in the morning. Linda headed for the main entrance, and a doorman tipped his hat to her and smiled as she passed.

"Good morning, miss, how are you today?"

"Fine, thank you." Linda replied hastily, eager to be on her way. It irritated her how everyone was so overly polite in expensive hotels.

She walked a few streets from the hotel and got into a cab and asked to be dropped off at the train station. Inside the station she headed for the restrooms. When she came out, she had become another person. She had abandoned her fine, expensive clothes for tattered, misfit ones. Her coat was torn in a few places, and it had buttons missing. It was too large for her and fell to within inches of the floor. On her head she wore a used black tuque that she had pulled down over her ears. Her eyes were hidden by a large pair of dark sunglasses that had probably been in style long before she was born. A dirty piece of white tape held the sunglasses together at the bridge. She wore a faded gray plaited shirt, black baggy pants, and a rundown pair of sports shoes. Her face, thus partially revealed, was a gruesome and scary sight to behold. People looked at her in shock when she passed by them, and they got out of her path. Linda was oblivious to their reactions as she headed toward the locker area; she rented a locker and stuffed her leather bag inside. She slowly made her way toward the street, very aware of the reaction of the people she crossed. Their shocked gazes and their unfeigned expressions of disgust spoke eloquently of their coldness and their shallowness. Not one of them seemed to have an afterthought about how she had gotten that way. To them she was a homeless, disfigured cripple and a pariah, and they sidestepped her with disdain and haste.

She ignored them as she made her way toward a shelter near skid row. She had grown used to the meanness and insensitivity of people. It was the way of the world, and it did not hurt her to be treated thus. The only sentiment that it raised in her was pity—pity not for herself, but for the people who looked at the exterior of a human being and drew definitive conclusions from what they saw.

Today, however, Linda couldn't have cared less about all that. She was on her way to see Red, her friend, and the thought of him made her smile. Red was a homeless person and an alcoholic. He had fried so many of his brain cells with bad alcohol that he could not even remember where he was from originally. He told Linda that for as far as he could remember, he had always been homeless. "Hell, Linda, I swear, I was born this way." Red's ideas and recollections might have been confused, but his heart wasn't. He had a good heart. Red and Linda had become friends. They had met at the shelter a number of years before, and Linda always spent time with him whenever she came to the city. She loved him and would see him as often as she could when she was around. They drank coffee and played chess together at the shelter as they waited for the free lunch to be served at noon. He was a good man, Red, as fine a man as Linda had ever met in her other life.

"Hi, Red," Linda shuffled into the first floor cafeteria where he was sitting with a coffee in front of him, staring blankly ahead. Red was a sight to behold; his head was bald except for a stray hair or two, and his nose was round and very red. All of his face was covered with busted veins and was potholed and had a very burgundy and unhealthy taint to it. He had enormous drooping bags under his permanently bloodshot eyes and was missing his two front teeth. As for the remaining ones, they were of various shades of an unsavory yellow or green. He had a three-or-four day-old gray stubble and only shaved when the shelter or someone gave him a razor and some shaving cream. His nose was definitely his most prominent characteristic, though, because of its size and its redness. That's how he had gotten his name. His fellow companions of vagrancy and alcohol, whose sense of *a propos* could certainly not be challenged, had baptized him thus, and the name had stuck. Red had told Linda that he couldn't even remember his real name and that it had been so long since anyone had called him by it, that if someone did, he probably wouldn't even know that they were talking to him.

"Hey, Linda," Red snapped out of his reverie. "What's up? You been up to no good again, eh?" He smiled, showing the gap made by the absence of his two front teeth.

"Yeah, plenty of no good Red, what about you?" Linda sat in front of him; she took her sunglasses off and put her cane to one side. It didn't bother her to be uncovered here. She felt safe, and nobody seemed to care much. Red was oblivious to that. He had long passed the point in his life experience when such things mattered. For him, to take into consideration someone's exterior appearance was an absurdity. What mattered to him was the heart and soul of a person, nothing else. He found it hard to find people who had a good heart and soul, but he knew that Linda was one of them. He couldn't have cared less about her crushed face, burnt skin, and artificial eye. When she talked to him, it was straight from the heart, and that was the only language he understood. As he would often say, "My brain may be fried, but my heart ain't."

"Oh not much, the usual, you know. I've been walkin' about a bit, keepin' out of people's way, mindin' my own business and all. Just, Gerry, though. I think he's onto me again. I'm pretty sure I saw him yesterday near the corner of 21st and Main, but my eyes ain't so good no more, so I'm not really sure." Gerry was Red's dead drinking buddy who'd been killed in a hit and run five years earlier. Red was convinced that Gerry followed him around and meant him no good. It was true that Red's eyesight was bad, but it was also true that Gerry was dead. Linda was convinced that Red's sightings of Gerry were his way of keeping him alive, probably because he missed him.

"You need glasses, Red. Gerry isn't around, you know that. Why don't you ask social services for a pair?" He made a gesture of refusal with his hands and face.

"To hell with them, Linda, I don't trust those people, none of them. Plus, they ask me all kinds of questions—names, numbers, address, I don't remember any of it. I hate papers, and I hate even more people who fill them out. So no, no glasses for Red. Anyway, I still see okay by me, to hell with that." Red fidgeted about in his seat, looking from left to right. The subject of being helped always upset him.

"Hey, Red, you know what? I brought you some of those jams you like so much." She retrieved some small jam jars from her bag that her hotel served every morning with breakfast; she always saved them for Red. She put them on the table, and Red rapidly scooped them up and put them in his overcoat pockets. He looked around furtively to make sure nobody had seen him. In the world of the have-nots, it is better not to show off something that could entice envy, and Red knew that even jam jars could do that.

"Thanks, Linda. Boy, that lady who gives these to you near the hotel sure is regular."

"Yeah, she sure is, regular and kind. You know what else, Red? I told her about you, about how you needed glasses and all and you know what she said to me?" Red eyed her quizzically; he did not like being the subject of conversations when he was not present.

"No, what?"

"She told me I should look out for you Red, you know, seeing as I'm your friend and all."

"She said that, eh," Red said and smiled absentmindedly.

"Yeah, she said that, Red, I swear she did."

"Well, that's mighty kind of her, but you don't have to look out for me, Linda." He leaned toward Linda with a wry smile on his face and a mischievous gleam in his eyes. "I can take care of myself good enough, you know. I've been around a long time," he whispered.

"Yeah, I know, Red, but hey, what do you say I watch your back and you watch mine, eh?" she whispered back.

"Yeah sure, Linda, I can do that." He leaned back and smiled content with their exchange. The conversation had reached the limit of Red's mental capacity to concentrate on a subject.

"Hey, Linda, what do you say we have a game now?" He didn't wait for her to answer but moved the chessboard that was set up beside him in front of both of them. His eyes were bright. The prospect of a chess game excited him. It was the one thing that he was good at, apart from surviving in his hostile environment, that is; he was, by some neurological incongruity and against all odds, an excellent chess player and won most of the time. His concentration when he played chess was extreme.

"Okay, Red, let's play. You know what? Today I have a feeling I'm gonna whip you." He winced a few times as he examined the chessboard with intensity, his eyes bulging wildly, darting gleefully from side to side; he did not respond, already completely absorbed in the anticipation of his first moves.

"Well, miss, how was your day?" Charles asked when he came to check in on Linda at six.

"The usual, Charles, uneventful and pleasant, I guess. And you how was your day?" Linda was sitting in a large armchair close to a window that overlooked the city.

"Excellent, miss. I had a great day, thank you. Is there anything in particular I should know for tomorrow?" The question was part of their routine. If Linda had decided that they would be going the next day, this would have been the time that she would tell him. She never gave him more than a few hours' notice, and he never got an indication as to where they would be going next until the very last minute. Charles did not mind this little cat and mouse game that he and Linda played; he enjoyed it as much as he enjoyed Linda's little peculiarities and eccentricities. He had gotten used to life on the road with her and had grown quite fond of it. It was pleasant enough, and he considered that he didn't have a very hard job.

"No, Charles, nothing in particular for tomorrow. So, what did you do today?"

"Well, I visited the museum. You know, they have a fabulous exhibition of African art—very complete, I might add. It took me a good three hours to do the whole tour. Then I headed down to the club. I've made some good friends down there, you know, British expatriates like me. We had a jolly time today, I'd say."

"Good for you, Charles. I'm glad you're enjoying your stay."

"Thank you, miss. Eating in, are you?" It was a superfluous question. Linda always ate in, and he knew that, but still, he liked to ask.

"Yes, Charles I'm eating in, thank you for asking."

"Well, if there's nothing else, I wish you a good evening, and I'll see you tomorrow, miss."

"Yes, good evening to you too, Charles. I'll see you tomorrow." He turned and left the room. Linda heard the whooshing and clicking of the door of the suite as it closed behind him.

She sat silently in the armchair for over an hour. She did not open the book sitting in her lap but stared out the window to the bustling city twenty stories below. From her vantage point, people were like ants, scurrying hurriedly about in a seemingly frantic and disorganized way. "How little time people take to reflect on the meaning of their lives," she pondered. Linda's gaze turned upward toward the cloudless sky. It was rapidly getting dark, and the horizon was ablaze with the crimson light of the dying sun. A profound melancholy suddenly invaded her, and for the first time in a long time she felt sad—sad and lonely, bitterly lonely. It was a loneliness so profound and so powerful that it caused her physical pain. Tears welled up in her eye and began to flow down her cheek. She clutched her chest with her one good hand and cried out loud, addressing the heavens, "Oh God, how could you have condemned me to this, how?" She thumped on her chest with her hand, and the tears continued to flow down her face. She began to shake, and tremors ran through her body. "Please help me, God, please." She had lowered her voice to a whisper, her gaze still pointing intently toward the darkening sky. She was startled by a knock on the door, and she turned around and quickly covered her head and veiled her face.

"Come in," she shouted, sitting upright in the semidarkness.

The door opened. It was Maria, the housekeeper, arriving with Linda's dinner.

"Hello, Miss Staunton, how are you tonight?" Maria was pushing a room service table and talking at the same time. She was a heavyset woman of Mexican origins, always cheerful and very religious. Maria had seven children, and she believed that each one of them was a gift from God.

"I'm fine, Maria; you're early tonight, aren't you?" Linda was still trembling from the powerful emotions that had just swept her body and was glad she was wearing a veil that concealed her distress.

"Oh no, I'm not, Miss Staunton, it's exactly seven o'clock." Her heavily accented voice pitched up and down and had a pleasant musicality to it.

"Oh really, I hadn't realized what time it was. I was lost in my thoughts, I guess. So, what have you brought me, my good Maria?"

"Only good things, miss, only good things." Maria's cheerfulness made Linda momentarily forget her forlornness and profound melancholy.

"I have fish, grilled, just like you like it, some steamed vegetables, and a small green salad." Maria was pointing to the various plates as she spoke. "Okay, here we go." Maria lit the lamp behind Linda, set up the table, and laid out the food.

"Now if you need anything else, you just call me, okay? I'll be back in an hour to pick everything up."

"Yes fine, Maria, thank you."

"You're welcome. I'll see you in a little while, then." Maria left the suite. When Maria would come back later to pick up the dishes, Linda would have her sit down and they would have tea together and chat. It had become a ritual between them every night that Maria was on duty. She was an endless source of stories and anecdotes and had a large family, and there was always something going on with somebody. Linda loved these little chats with Maria. She was the only person in this five-star hotel, or any five-star hotel, as a matter of fact, that she could really relate to. Maria was a warm, loving, and caring person who was authentic and who had never fabricated an emotion or told a lie in her whole life. Linda had told her about herself in detail and about her accident and her subsequent recovery. Maria had sympathized with her and had never brought it up again. She treated Linda like any other human being and was oblivious to her condition.

Regular as clock work, Maria showed up exactly an hour later carrying a tea tray and some cookies.

"I'm telling you, Miss Staunton, my brother nearly had a heart attack," she began even before sitting down. "His own son doing a thing like that, can you imagine?" The day before she had been telling Linda about her nephew, Carlos, who had been arrested for drunk driving. Maria was shocked by the boy's behavior.

"That boy, he's always in trouble, I told Ernesto, Ernesto, you have to be more strict with the boys, because boys, they're full of crazy ideas in their heads. But who listens to me, heh? Nobody, that's the problem, nobody listens to Maria. After all who am I, eh? I've only put seven children into the world, with God's help, of course." Maria looked upward and did a sign of the cross. On and on she went. She was a fountain of exuberance. Life gushed from her as water from a mountain stream. To her nothing was unimportant or trivial and everything mattered. Her generous nature and stories of ordinary people living their day-to-day lives brought some much-needed humanity into Linda's solitary existence.

After Maria left, Linda picked up her book again. Although she could only read for a few hours at a time because her eye became tired, books had become her passion. She had begun reading the classics thanks to Charles's excellent advice; he brought her more books than she could read, and she devoured them with an uncommon rage. Linda could not concentrate on reading tonight, however, and there was no book in the world that could have chased away her catastrophic solitude and the hollow, empty feeling inside her heart.

The next day at the shelter, Linda put a package on the table of the cafeteria in front of Red.

"What's that?" he asked, looking at her suspiciously.

"It's a present, Red, from that lady, remember? I told you about her, the one that gives me the jam jars."

"A present, what for, she doesn't even know me?" He eyed the package but did not reach for it.

"Yes, but I do, and she asked me to give this to you," she pushed the package in his direction. He eyed her, itching to grab the package but resisting.

"Go on; take it; its okay," Linda encouraged him.

Slowly Red opened the package. Inside were some reading glasses, a new pair of gloves, some stockings, and a large woolen sweater. All were items he needed and that would make his life a little more comfortable. He examined each item attentively, trying on the glasses and the gloves, obviously satisfied.

"I don't really need these glasses, you know, Linda, but I'll keep them just in case, okay?"

"Yeah, okay, Red."

"That's mighty kind of that lady, Linda. You make sure you say thank you for me, will you?" He wrapped everything up quickly and placed the package at his feet under the table, looking around for prying eyes.

"I will, Red. I'll tell her. She gave me something else for you, Red, but I don't want you to open it until you're alone, okay?" Very discretely Linda took out an envelope from her bag; in it she had put fifty twenty-dollar bills. She looked about furtively left and right like he did all the time. "Put this in your pocket right away," she whispered. In a swift movement, she handed him the envelope, and he snatched it from her hand and put it hastily in his inside jacket pocket, looking about with a silly smile on his face as if he had just stolen the last cookie from the cookie jar. He rubbed his hands together and looked toward Linda gleefully.

"Okay, can we play now, Linda?" Not waiting for a reply, he placed the chessboard in front of them and began placing the pieces on it.

"Yeah, Red, we can play." Linda was happy; she knew she had made his life a little better, even if it would only be for a short time.

That evening Linda told Charles they were leaving the next morning and to get everything ready. Charles did not ask her where they were going; he knew he would only find out in the morning.

For seven years Linda and Charles traveled across the country, going from city to city. Some cities they visited a number of times and others they never went back to. There was no particular plan; they would sometimes stay two weeks in one place and then three months in the next. Linda kept in touch with her family by phone, social media and by email. She spoke to her mother often, but in all those years, she had never gone back home and had seen no one of her family since Peggy's wedding. Linda just could not bear the thought of being around them; they were all getting on with their lives, which were filled with jobs, children, and beautiful homes. The thought of finding herself in the midst of all that life and joy was, to her, simply unbearable. She considered herself a burden because of her condition, and she felt that it was better that she stay away. Her mother found this very hard to deal with, but she knew there was nothing she could do or say that would make Linda change her mind. She hoped that one day she would relent and come and visit them. She sent Linda pictures and videos of every baby and of every birthday party and of every Christmas or family reunion. She had the little ones draw her pictures and write her notes, and she made sure that Linda remained a part of their lives. Linda sent them presents and cards on birthdays and at Christmas, and she talked to all of them on the phone, but still, she stayed away.

The road had become Linda's new family; she loved the anonymity and the detachment inherent to always being on the move. No one could get close to her or enter her intimacy—no one except Charles, that is. He was her anchor and her savior; he took care of her with infinite tenderness and attention and was discreet and kind and gentle and considerate. When it came to her comfort, he would check things to the tiniest detail, as if his own life depended on it. They had become close in many ways, yet at the same time they remained strangers. It was the way they were together. It was not something that they had decided or wished, but the way things had worked themselves out for them.

Linda continued to explore the world of the homeless and the abandoned in every city she went. She became much bolder in what she did; she wore clothes that were more and more decrepit, and on a few occasions, she had even uncovered her face completely on busy streets and in broad daylight. The repulsive reactions of people fascinated her. They sidestepped her as if she was contagious, grim expressions on their faces, and mothers protectively pushed their children aside, covering their eyes so they could not see her. Sometimes Linda would stretch out an open hand to them, a few put some coins in her hand, but most just walked by hurriedly, eyes averted, unwilling to have any form of contact with her.

The only people who did not shun her were the street people, the homeless and the vagrants and the ones that society had permanently put aside. These people continued to fascinate her. She wanted to know more about them, about their world and their lives and about what made them who they were, about where they came from, and how they had ended up on the street. During the day she wandered their streets of predilection and visited their haunts. She hung out at the parks that they hung out in, and she lived and breathed by the rules of the street. Amongst the street people she became indistinguishable. They immediately accepted her into their midst. To them she was just another person with a sad story to tell. Linda loved to move about their unforgiving and dangerous world. She felt that she belonged there. It was among the have-nots and the destitute that she recovered her fractured sense of self, and it was when she was among them that her heart filled up again with love and hope.

"So, miss, I hope this is going to be a long drive." It was a beautiful, clear summer day, and they had just hit the road.

"I guess so Charles, why?"

"Well, I feel like driving today. The sun is out, and the road is opening its arms to us, and we haven't been on the road for months, you know I kind of missed it."

"Me too, Charles, I missed it too." Linda stared out the window at the countryside rolling past, allowing her thoughts to wander. After a short while she looked up front toward Charles.

"Charles?"

"Yes, miss?"

"Tell me, do you believe in God?"

"Why do you ask, miss?"

"Oh I don't know, curious I guess."

"Okay, miss, let's see; where should I start? Well, the first thing I'd say is that I have a lot of difficulty imagining some kind of superior being who is aware and who cares about what's going on in the lives of billions of human beings. That for me is a preposterous notion, as is heaven and hell, reincarnation, or any other fairy tale that was invented by the priests, rabbis, imams, and so on. These self-proclaimed men of God invented these stories in a time when people did not know how to read or write and practically all knowledge or news was transmitted orally. They feverishly pitched their visions as absolute truths to ignorant and uneducated masses. Those were brutal times in human history, miss; people did not live very long, because of wars, disease, or famines. Most societies were ruled by absolute power, and religion was the tool that the kings and demagogues used to keep the masses in check. The men of God gratefully obliged them, and God became the answer to everything and to anything." Charles was on fire, gesticulating with his hands and body, his eyes moving from the road to the rearview mirror, where he could see Linda listening in silence in the back of the car. If he could have seen beneath her veil, he would have noticed that she had a bemused smile on her face.

"The organized religions of today are the remnants of what has been passed down to us from that past. They are all destined for the historical junkyard, miss, and the reason is very simple; they have become obsolete, and education and the development of our collective intellect will bury them." Charles paused for a moment, and Linda smiled and said, "Wow, Charles, it was just a question. I didn't expect a lecture." Charles did not heed her comment. Linda had got him going and now, and he was on roll.

"But you see, on the other hand, miss, when I observe the magnitude of the universe and the beauty of this planet, I stand in awe of that. I am humbled and silenced by all that magnificence and the mystery of our existence. So, what do I believe in? I believe that we are minuscule inhabitants of the universe, no more important than any other inhabitants of the universe that might be out there, and as for understanding the mysteries of the universe and how we got here and where this is all going, well, it's not something that I think I will find out in my lifetime, so I don't dwell on it."

"Amen, Charles, amen," Linda liked the way Charles put things. She did not always agree with him, but she liked his analytical mind and methodical explanations and the fact that he always tried to go to the bottom of things.

"There is, however, one thing, miss, that comes close to making me a believer." Charles was not done with the subject yet.

"Oh yeah, and what may that be?"

"Music, miss, music is the most thrilling and exciting thing that humans have ever created. When I hear a beautiful piece of music, it rushes through my being like a surge of electricity and then, I swear, I almost believe in God."

"Oh really? Well that's an interesting way to put it. I'm sure that God would be happy to hear that." Charles chuckled, and they fell silent for a moment. Linda stared out the window, her mind wandering off.

"I don't believe in God either, Charles. Sometimes I pray to this entity called God, but I don't believe in it. It's like talking to myself, you know? I guess we all need to validate our thoughts to something or someone. I think a lot of people probably don't want to know if God exists or not. It would screw up their lives either way. I think God is only a word, an expression to describe things that are beyond our comprehension. People need to believe, Charles; they need to believe in something, no matter how preposterous or unbelievable it might sound. It's as essential as breathing for them. It's strange, really, when you think about it. It makes no sense, yet it does, you know, in a way. Sometimes, it's so bloody confusing; it's easy to get lost." She turned from staring out the window and looked up; she could see that he was nodding his head gravely in approval.

"Your sure right about that, Miss, it can certainly be confusing. You see, the way I see things is this, in a practical sense, I mean. The time we have, I mean the time that we are alive, well, that's the only thing that counts really, because that's all we have. We have the obligation to make the most of that and to be respectful of others and of all living things, including the planet. You know, I read a quotation once, and I cannot even remember from whom it was, but it struck me at the time. It went something like this, *"Plan your life as if you'll live forever, but live it as if you'll die tomorrow."*

"Right on Charles, I can relate to that, believe me I can."

"Yes you can, miss, you certainly can."

They both fell silent, lost in their own thoughts. Their conversations were the best part of their travels as they drove through the countryside. They always took the secondary roads so as to go through the small towns and villages at a nice slow pace. They had mutually agreed to abandon freeways and highways years before. Because they spent whole days in close proximity, they talked a lot, about every subject under the sun. Charles was an excellent conversationalist, and he was educated, brilliant, and well read. Linda was a good listener, and she could hold up her own on any subject. To the farmers and country people they passed along the way, they must have been a most unusual sight, a black foreign limo passing slowly by with a veiled woman sitting upright in the back seat, engaged in a vivid conversation with a large, broad-shouldered black man who was driving and gesticulating vigorously with his hands at the same time. Both of them, apparently oblivious to their surroundings and to the people they were passing by.

"Have you ever been married, Charles?" Linda had ventured a personal question once.

"Once, miss, when I was a young man. I was twenty at the time, back home, you know." Although Linda immediately felt that the subject was a sensitive one, curiosity got the better of her.

"Well, Charles, what happened?" Charles looked at her one or two times in the rearview mirror before answering. The question had caught him off guard, and he was pondering what he was going to say.

"Well, the short version goes this way, miss. We met when we were in our teens, and we really hit it off from the very first day. You know, love at first sight and all that. We were glued together, inseparable; we swore to each other that we would spend the rest of our lives together. That's the way things were and we got married right after our graduation. Nothing fancy, you know. We were so in love and so anxious to be a legitimate couple." Charles cleared his throat; his voice was higher pitched than usual; speaking about this chapter of his life was obviously stirring up some long-forgotten emotions. "Well anyway, the marriage lasted four years, and all seemed good and in its place, at least to me. Then one day I got home from work and she wasn't there and there was a note on the kitchen counter. In it she explained to me that she was gone for good because she needed to find herself and to start a new life. She admitted she didn't have the courage to tell me face to face, and she thought it would be easier for both of us this way. I couldn't believe she had dumped me, just like that, without a warning. I really hadn't seen that coming, and it hit me hard. I was shattered and devastated. It was only a few days later that I found out that she had run off with another guy, but she hadn't mentioned that in the note, of course. Nor did she mention that the other guy was my very best friend. Well anyway, I never saw either one of them again. It was the worst time of my life, miss, and the bitterest lesson I ever had to learn." Charles was staring intently at the road ahead, obviously disturbed by the memories of that time in his life. Linda knew she shouldn't ask the next question, but she felt compelled to.

"You mean that you can never trust another woman ever again, in that way, I mean. Is that the lesson you learned, Charles?"

"Well, yes and no, miss. Of course, I've had major trust issues with woman since then. I mean, who could blame me? You see, the most important thing I learned is to never take anyone for granted, because they could be there one day and gone the next. I know that now, but at the time, I felt only pain, and I suffered a very long time because of her." His voice was charged with emotion, and he seemed to be on the verge of tears. Linda moved into the seat behind him and put her hand on his shoulder.

"What was her name, Charles?" she asked softly.

"Susan," he whispered. "Susan Spencer," he repeated, his eyes glued straight ahead.

"I'm sure that deep down she was a wonderful person, Charles, and I'm sorry that I brought this up. I shouldn't have, I'm sorry."

"It's okay, miss, all that happened a long time ago now." They both fell silent; Linda patted his shoulder and returned to her seat.

A bond had been created between them that day. Charles had revealed his most painful and intimate secrets to her, and Linda felt closer to him than she ever had before. He could have asked her about her own experience with love that

163

day. After all, she was the one who had brought the subject up, but he hadn't, and Linda had felt relieved about that. She would have hated to have to tell him about her own sad saga and the seething pain it had inflicted on her so many years before. Thoughts of Richard flooded her mind, and with it came the memories of her broken heart and the countless nights she had cried herself to sleep. She found it painful to even think about the past, not to mention her present situation, which, in her mind, excluded anything that could resemble a relationship of any sorts.

On the road they ate together most of the time now. Linda had pleaded with Charles intensely and he had finally relented. The small hotels or motels they stayed at always had a dining room or a diner nearby. Linda enjoyed those meals a lot. Charles had fine table manners and excellent taste, attributes that she appreciated greatly. They were having dinner in a small diner one night when Charles put down his fork and knife and cleared his throat.

"May I ask you a question, miss?" Charles loved to ask permission to do things, even ask a question. Linda looked up from her plate.

"Yes, of course, Charles, please do."

"Do you have any idea how many more years we'll be on the road, miss? I mean, we've been roaming the country for quite a while now, so I thought I might venture to ask." Linda pondered her reply for a moment.

"I don't know, Charles, but I promise you one thing. As soon as I do know, you'll be the first to be informed." Linda's deformed face broke into a half-smile under her veil, and Charles detected a nuance of mischief in her tone.

"Well, thank you miss that was a very enlightening reply. I will sleep better tonight now that you have shed some light on our mysterious wanderings." There was a moment of silence and then he broke out laughing, a loud, hearty laugh, and so did she. The other patrons of the diner turned their heads in their direction, but Charles and Linda paid no attention to them. It just felt too good to laugh. Of course, hidden in their outburst of laughter was the fact that Linda had not answered his question. The simple truth was that she did not know how long they would be traveling, but the question had been haunting her of late.

They arrived in the big city after three weeks on the road—three weeks of back roads and rolling country, of quaint villages filled with simple people going about their quiet lives. Linda always felt that these incursions into the rural areas of the country were like a balm. There was something endearing and appeasing about it all, and in a way, it was reassuring for her to know that places and people like this existed. It felt good and wholesome, like a glass of cold, fresh milk at the end of a hot summer day.

She and Charles had taken their time and made their way slowly toward the city, but now, they were there at last. It was a familiar city, the biggest in the country, embodying the best and worst of everything, and Linda's favorite. They had been there numerous times over the years, and although Linda loved the country, she needed the city more and this city, above all others. She needed its strength and its power and its vitality and its urgency. It was different from the other cities they had been to. It had its own essence and its own soul, throbbing with the effervescence and excitement of life in eruption, clashing against itself in an endless explosion of beauty and brutality and changing instantaneously, to the whims of its intrinsic complexity. It was dirty and clean, violent but peaceful, articulate yet dysfunctional, frightening yet reassuring. It was everything, and yet, at the same time, it was nothing but the sum of its inhabitants and their tumultuous, intertwining lives.

When Linda was there, walking its streets in her homeless attire, weaving amongst its vibrant throngs and drowning in the dizziness of its din, she felt that it was like living inside a heart.

They checked into the hotel at about ten at night.

"Good evening, Miss Staunton, it's nice to see you again. It's been a while, hasn't it?"

The hotel employee who had opened the car door was all over them. Linda remained silent behind her veil, and as usual in such circumstances, she let Charles do the talking.

"A year, Henry, it's been a year. We want to check in quickly, Henry; Miss Staunton is very tired from the trip and wishes to retire immediately."

"Yes, of course, Mr. Charles. We just need to get you signed in at the reception. It will take two minutes at the most, and you'll be upstairs." Henry directed them toward the reception, and Linda signed them in hastily, and then she and Charles headed toward the elevator. A few minutes after they had entered Linda's suite, there was a knock on the door. It was Henry with the luggage. Charles showed him where to drop the suitcases and then tipped him.

"Thank you, Miss Staunton, Mr. Charles. I hope you have a pleasant stay with us, and if there's anything you need while you're here, anything whatsoever, I'll be glad to be of service. Good night now." He headed toward the door.

"Thank you, Henry, good night." Charles had followed him and closed the door behind him. He walked back toward Linda.

"Well, miss, if you don't need me anymore, I think I'll retire."

"No, I'm fine, Charles, thank you and good night."

"Good night, miss."

The next day Linda called Peggy. They had been keeping in touch regularly, but they had not seen each other since Peggy's wedding.

"Hi, Peggy, its' me."

"Oh hi, Linda, it's so nice to hear your voice. How have you been?"

"I'm good, thanks, and you?"

"I'm fine—great, actually. The kids are driving me crazy, though, but apart from that, all is good." Peggy had two children. Mark was one and a half, and Carrie was four.

"I'm sure you spoil them rotten and probably love them too much."

"Yeah, I do. It's just that they're so bloody adorable, I can't help myself. I wish you could see them, though, I mean, besides the pictures and the videos, you know, like seeing them in person."

"I will, Peggy. Someday I will, I promise, okay?"

"Promises, promises," Peggy said sarcastically. Linda did not respond, so Peggy changed the subject.

"So, what have you been up to?"

"Oh, you know the usual. Moving around, discovering new places." Linda lied; the truth was that she'd been getting more and more disenchanted with her traveling life of late. There was a touch of melancholy in her voice, and Peggy quickly detected it.

"Really," she said, sounding skeptical. "Well, I do hope you settle down someday. It would be good for you to have a home and a place of your own. You should be around people who love you, Linda. I worry about you. Don't you get lonely sometimes?"

"Stop it, Peggy, will you? You sound like my mother, for God's sake. I'm surrounded by people, okay? And no, I don't have time to be lonely; there are always tons of things going on. Charles and I have our little routine. Believe me, we're very busy and everything is fine." She'd slightly raised her voice, thus revealing how sensitive the subject was. Peggy remained unconvinced.

"Oh come on, Linda, how many times have you been around the country? Haven't you had enough of this constant moving around? It can't be good for you; you need to settle down, Linda. Promise me you'll think about it?"

"Okay, Peggy, I will. I promise, okay?" They dropped the subject, but the truth was that Linda had been thinking a lot about abandoning the road lately. She was growing more and more restless with her bohemian life. It was not bringing her the satisfaction that it used to. She wasn't ready to share those thoughts with Peggy, though, and she didn't really want to admit to her that she didn't really know what to do with her life.

They talked for over an hour, exchanging news about each other's families, Peggy was a talker, and she would describe even the smallest family incident with infinite detail. Linda loved to listen to her. She made her laugh, and not many people did that in her life. There were no boyfriends or husbands or children to talk about on Linda's end, and it was a subject that they stayed away from. They said good-bye after Peggy made Linda promise that she would visit soon, a promise that both of them knew she wouldn't keep. Linda didn't visit anyone. She didn't visit her family, and she wouldn't visit Peggy either. That's the way things were. The worst part was that the more Linda stayed away from them, the more she dreaded the very idea of having to face any of them ever again.

The next morning was a bright and sunny summer day. Linda left the hotel early and took a taxi to the train station, carrying her used leather bag. When she got there she went into the restrooms and changed into her homeless outfit, putting her clean clothes into the bag. She walked out of the restrooms in the direction of the lockers for rent and rented a locker and put her bag into it. She then left the station and headed toward St. Mary's Mission, which was a few streets away. Her pace was fast, considering that she walked with a cane. Linda was in a hurry today, in a hurry to see her friend Janice, whom she had not seen in over a year. She couldn't help but notice how people balked and were repulsed by her as she passed them by. Linda couldn't have cared less, though; people's reactions to her appearance and her disfigurement didn't bother her anymore.

St. Mary's Mission was a large four-story brown brick building that was located in the middle of the seedier part of the city. It was an area of cheap rooms and cheap booze, where prostitutes and junkies roamed the streets day and night. The buildings were decrepit, and the streets were dirty, like the inhabitants of the numerous missions and shelters of the area. Linda felt comfortable among them, the street people and the have nothing people. This area was their haven and their lair. It belonged to them, the hookers and the druggies, the lost and the abandoned, the mentally ill and the winos, the idiots and the bums, the disillusioned and the misguided, the criminals and the rejected. It was strangely in places like these that Linda had reconnected with herself and where she had found her bearings again. They had become safe havens for her, and she felt that she was among her own.

She made her way with difficulty up the stairs of the Mission. St. Mary's Mission was a shelter that opened its doors at 5:00 p.m. every day to those men or woman who needed a bed for the night. Everyone who showed up was given clean underwear, socks, a hot meal, a towel, and a toothbrush. No drugs or alcohol were allowed, and all had to take a shower before going to bed. Lights out was at 10:00 p.m. and wake up was at 6:00 a.m. Breakfast was served at seven, and at nine everyone was put back out on the street. No one was refused here; the nuns who ran the place welcomed everyone. The only time people were turned away was when the mission had reached its capacity. It was sadly something that seemed to happen more and more often of late, much to the chagrin of the nuns. If someone was intoxicated on anything, he or she was turned away. All the employees who helped the nuns run the place were ex-street people who lived at the mission full time. They knew their customers well and had a sharp eye out for troublemakers. Linda thought it was one of the best shelters she had seen, and she had seen many in the course of her travels. Not only was it clean, but it was also well run. People could say what they wanted about the nuns; they ran a tight ship and were dedicated and hardworking.

Linda entered the cafeteria on the ground floor, which stayed open all day and served free coffee and cookies. There were a few people there, but Linda did not see her friend Janice. She headed to the reception, where an ex-junkie called Rick was tending the phone and shuffling some paper. Rick did not have a square inch on his arms that was not tattooed. His face was ravaged from childhood acne and scared from many vicious street and prison fights.

"Hi." Rick didn't look up; he was staring at a document, obviously having difficulty with what it said or didn't say. Linda waited; she knew that impatience was not well accepted in this world. After a few minutes, he put the document down and got up. Looking in Linda's direction, he nodded his head, acknowledging her presence.

"Hi, what can I do for you?" Linda's deformities and appearance did not seem to disturb him in any way.

"I'm looking for Janice—you know, crazy Janice." Linda looked upward, imitating her friend.

"Yeah, I know Janice." They called Janice that because she walked the streets of the city looking up, never down, never ahead, but up. Although her upward gaze never flinched, she would never bump into anybody or anything, which was, all things considered, an amazing feat in itself and quite a sight to behold. People had nicknamed her Crazy Janice ages ago because of that peculiar habit. Everyone took it for granted that she had lost her mind. Linda knew better.

"She was here last night, left early this morning." He looked straight into Linda's eye, gaze unwavering, obviously not intimidated by her, as a lot of people might have been.

"Do you know where I can find her?"

"Yeah, I suppose I do." He answered, saying nothing else. Linda knew that obtaining information in this world required trust.

"I'm an old friend of hers, and I haven't seen her in a long time. I've been away, you know?" Linda pointed with her thumb behind her in the direction of the street and looked upwards, indicating by these gestures that she'd been somewhere unpleasant and on an involuntary basis.

"Oh yeah," Rick nodded with understanding eyes, certain that Linda had just been released from jail or from an asylum, which made her trustworthy in his book. "She's usually in the park about noon; she goes there to feed the pigeons."

"Thanks." Linda smiled to him; he did not return her smile but sat back down and resumed what he had been doing.

Linda made her way to the park. It was still early, and she sat down on a park bench enjoying the warm summer day. Everything was green and lush, and the birds were chirping about noisily. She breathed in deeply and closed her eye for a few moments, absorbing the odors of the park and the noises of the city. Although she was a stranger here, Linda felt like she had a bond to the city and that it was like coming home in a way. There was something about being here that filled her with excitement, and there seemed to be an inherent promise of fulfillment built into its very fiber, and it felt good to be back.

Linda stayed a few hours sitting on the park bench, taking in the nature and watching people go by. Then, a little before noon, she saw Janice approaching from the other side of the park. Janice wore a knee-length green wool coat and beige leggings; her shoes were black and had thick two-inch heels. They were hand-me-downs from the nuns and made a distinct clicking sound when she walked. She wore the same attire she had on when Linda had last seen her over a year before. She walked with one hand clinging to the top of her coat, as if she were cold, and the other one buried deep in one of her coat pockets. Her long brownish hair was disheveled and fell below her shoulders; she was tall and wiry, and one could sense in her gait that she had an uncommon nervousness about her. She walked briskly up the path, humming to herself, as was her habit, her pale blue eyes fixed upward and steady. She stopped when she got near the fountain and pulled out a paper bag from her coat pocket. She fished some breadcrumbs from the bag and began to throw them all around her. Soon the pigeons were flocking at her feet. Linda observed her for a minute or two, and then she got up and slowly made her way to where Janice was standing.

"Come on, my little babies, there you go. My God, you're hungry," Janice was encouraging her friends, the pigeons, as they noisily devoured the breadcrumbs. She was looking at them affectionately. Her head was in a normal position when she was not walking. For some reason, she only kept it up when she walked.

"Janice," Linda now stood a few feet behind her; Janice turned and looked at her and then returned to feeding the pigeons.

"Where've you been? I thought you were dead or something." Janice spoke with her back to Linda, and there was a taint of reproach in her voice.

"I've been away, Janice, you know ... away." Linda hesitated for a few seconds. "And you, how've you been?"

"Okay I guess." Linda's laconic explanation seemed to satisfy her. Janice knew all too well that people were often sent to jail or to institutions for extended periods of time.

"Hey, Janice, want to come and sit with me on the bench over there? I've got some sandwiches, and we could share them if you want." Janice continued to feed the pigeons and did not answer. After a few moments she turned around and said,

"Okay," she pointed her head upward and began to walk toward the bench that Linda had indicated. Linda shuffled behind her. They sat in silence for a while, eating the sandwiches and observing the noisy feeding pigeons.

"So, you okay now?" Janice asked, turning toward Linda.

"Yeah, I'm okay. I'm good." Linda smiled, and Janice turned to look at the feeding pigeons again.

"Good, I'm glad you're okay."

Janice had spent her life in and out of mental institutions, ever since she had been diagnosed at twenty-one as a schizophrenic. For over twelve years, she had been going from the street to an institution and vice versa. Linda had noticed her the very first time she had come in the area, and she had approached her. Janice had taken no heed of Linda's condition, and they had become friends, spending a lot of time together. Linda had been secretly helping her for years. She gave money to the nuns for Janice, and they made sure that she always had the things she needed when Linda was away.

"You gonna be around for a while this time?" Janice asked, with a touch of anxiety in her voice.

"As long as I can, Janice, I promise, okay?"

"Okay, sure."

"What about you? You doing okay?"

"Yeah, I guess so, Linda. I like to feed the pigeons a lot, you know. They're nice, and they don't make fun of me."

"That's good, Janice; it's very nice of you to take care of the pigeons like that."

"Do you think they recognize me, Linda?"

"I'm sure they do. You bring them food, and they know that. They must love you very much, Janice." Janice shuffled her feet and looked to the ground, as if she was embarrassed by the thought that anyone or anything could love her.

They passed the rest of the afternoon together. Slowly Janice opened up and told Linda all of the latest stories of the very particular world she lived in—the one around her and the one inside her head. Linda loved to listen to Janice. She was sensitive and a lot smarter than most people in her surroundings imagined she was. Her descriptions of the characters of the street and their lives were unique and filled with nuances and savory details. Although some chemical or electrical imbalance in her brain had made her different, she could be brilliant and articulate and was far from stupid. Linda was convinced that her looking up routine was just that—a routine and a defense mechanism. It was her way of keeping undesirable people away from her. Janice and Linda had been friends ever since they met. They both felt comfortable in each other's presence, and neither one of them was bothered by the other's particularities. Linda looked toward Janice affectionately and smiled. Janice smiled back, and Linda put her scared and deformed hand on Janice's white elongated one.

"I missed you, you know." Janice smiled and stared to the ground, moving her feet about nervously under the bench. Linda slowly got up.

"I've got to go now, Janice."

"Oh yeah," Janice got up too. "Will I see you tomorrow, Linda?" she looked toward her with a worried expression on her face.

"I'll come and see you feed the pigeons, I promise, okay?"

"Okay then. Bye now, see you tomorrow." Without another word, Janice looked up to the sky and walked away at a rapid pace, her green coat flapping in the breeze and her thick black shoes attacking the pavement methodically as she went.

Linda began to walk away slowly, and she did not see the man across the park that had been observing her. Charles had seen everything, but then again, he had been observing Linda's incursions into the worlds of the homeless for many years now. He knew all about her daytime activities, about where she went, who she knew, and who she gave money to or tried to help. Charles was a meticulous man, and he considered it his job to know everything about his employer. He had never told Linda that he knew about her double life out of respect for her. She had chosen not to tell him, and he would never let on that he knew. If she wanted to communicate this information to him at any given time and for whatever reason, or if she decided never to tell him, that would be fine by him. He would deal with either situation with circumspection and professionalism. In the meantime, he considered it his job to follow her around and to make sure that no harm came her way. Linda entered the train station, and Charles, who had been following her at a safe distance, took a different direction and headed back to the hotel.

Two months went by this way. Linda would see Janice every day at the park, and she brought her food and gave her small amounts of money. They chatted and fed the pigeons together. It was the best part of Linda's day. When she was with Janice or out and about as a homeless person, she felt whole and alive again. She was filled with a sense of freedom and came as close to feeling happy again as she had ever been since her accident.

At night, however, alone in her luxury suite, things were different. She was crushed and suffocated by her loneliness, and she had come to dread the evenings she spent alone. She would take a few glasses of wine after dinner to try to alleviate her turmoil, but because of the medications she still took, it had an adverse effect on her. The alcohol compounded her misery and brought her immense solitude to the surface, invading her as suddenly as the powerful waves of a tsunami coming into shore, flooding her with its force and rummaging about her soul as a relentless tormentor. The pain inside her would make her stand up, because she found it difficult to breathe, and she would engage in an intoxicated monologue, addressing the heavens and herself.

"All the luxury and wealth in the world can't take the place of a human being, Linda," she shouted. "What's life without love, Linda? Not much really, is it now?" She took another sip of wine, her intoxicated gaze frozen on the city below. "What is life if you can't share your emotions and dreams with someone you love? Good question, eh, Linda, good question; nothingness, emptiness, and solitude, Linda, that's what you've been served. That's what you've been given and nothing else." The glass of wine slipped from her hand and fell with a thud on the thickly carpeted floor, splashing the blood of the earth unto the rich carpet. Tears began to pour down her face, and her body began to shake as the pain hit her in relentless waves. She looked upward toward the star-lit sky and wailed, "Please, God, show me the way. I can't do this anymore, I just can't." The tears kept coming and the melancholy that inhabited her invaded her heart and soul and took control of her broken body with the viciousness of a predator finishing off its prey. She slowly made her way to the bedroom and fell writhing on the bed, whining like a hurt animal, consumed by her pain, until finally blissful sleep came to deliver her from her immeasurable misery.

The phone woke her; it seemed to have been ringing forever. Linda turned on the light and looked at the clock. It was 5:00 a.m. She was still fully dressed from the night before. She picked up,

"Hello." Her voice was cracked and laden with sleep and alcohol.

"Hi, Linda, it's Veronica."

"Veronica, its five a.m., what's going on?" Linda became worried; her sister calling her at this hour was most unusual.

"It's Mama, Linda, she's sick, very sick and now the doctors say she won't make it. You have to come right away, Linda. You have to come as fast as you can." Veronica broke into tears, letting out a low whining sound.

Linda sat up. She was fully awake now.

"Veronica, what are you talking about? She was okay when I spoke to her last week."

"No she wasn't, Linda. She didn't want you to know, that's all. She's been sick for three years now. She has cancer, and they treated her, and for a while it was looking good, but in the past months things have turned for the worse. The cancer has spread very rapidly in the past few days, and now she's in the hospital. They admitted her last night, and they've put her on morphine, you know, for the pain. You have to come quickly, Linda." Veronica's tear-filled voice left no doubt about the urgency of the situation.

Linda was in complete shock. She could not imagine the world without her mother, her guardian angel, her everything, she who had always been there for her and had protected her and nurtured her through her darkest hours; she who had put her into the world with her pain; she who was her flesh and blood; she without whom she would be as a rudderless ship. The very thought of losing her felt like the end of the world to Linda. She began to tremble on the edge of the bed, and she felt queasy and weak.

"Oh God, Veronica, oh God," Linda began to cry too.

"I'm sorry to have to break this to you this way, Linda, but the hospital called me an hour ago and told me to expect the worst. I went over to Mom's house and found this hotel number to call you. She's asleep now; I'm going back over there in an hour. Please come quickly, Linda."

"Okay, I'll be there as fast as I can, Veronica, okay?"

"Okay, Linda, fine. I'll see you in a little while then."

"Yes, bye now." They both hung up, and Linda dialed Charles's room. The phone rang twice, and he picked up.

"Hello," his voice was hoarse.

"Charles, hi, sorry to wake you, but we must pack our bags and leave immediately. My mother is very sick. I have to get there as quickly as possible. Please hurry."

It took only a split second for Charles to understand the gravity of the situation; the professional in him took over quickly.

"Yes, miss, give me thirty minutes, forty-five at the most, and we're out of here."

"Thank you, Charles." Linda hung up, and she got out of bed and began to pack with incredible speed. "Don't let her die, God. Please, don't let her die until I get there. You owe me that, okay? Don't do this to me; just let me get there, okay? Just let me get there." Linda kept repeating the same thing out loud as she hastily threw her things into her suitcases.

Chapter 4

COMING HOME

The seven-hour drive from the city had been very silent. Linda and Charles had left the hotel suddenly less than an hour after Linda had received the phone call from her sister. Linda was nervous and agitated and had a knot in her stomach. The prospect of seeing her mother diminished and dying made her feel nauseous. At about one that afternoon, Charles hastily parked the car near the hospital's front door; Linda had decided to go there directly. She adjusted her hat, veil, and scarf and got out of the car. As hastily as she could, she made her way up the steps and headed toward the reception. Charles followed her a few steps behind.

Her mother was in a room at the far end of the fourth-floor corridor. The door was open. Linda stood in the doorway, hesitant, observing the scene for a moment. By her mother's bedside were Veronica, Dawn, and Derek. Dawn was the one who saw her first, and she walked over to greet her.

"Linda, it's Linda." Dawn took Linda's hand and placed it on her cheek and smiled.

"Oh, Linda, I'm so glad that you're here." She let go of Linda's hand and took her in her arms. Linda remained rigid; it had been years since another human being had hugged her.

"Come quickly, Linda, she's been asking for you," she guided Linda toward the bed where her mother lay. She was a sorry sight to see. Her body had shriveled, eaten away by the cancer, bones stuck out everywhere from under her whitish blue skin, and her cheeks and eyes were sunk deep into her head; she was obviously dying and in the last moments of her life. A flicker of light came into her eyes when she recognized Linda.

"Linda," she managed to say, her voice was feeble and more of a croak than anything else. Linda sat on the edge of the bed and took her emaciated hand in hers; she leaned down toward her and lifted her veil.

"Mama, Mama, I'm here now, I'm here." Linda smiled to her and held onto her hand tightly.

"I love you, Linda, I love you," she managed to say with her extinguished voice.

"Oh, Mama, I love you too. Why didn't you tell me, Mama, why?"

Her mother didn't answer; she smiled and let out a long sigh and life departed from her body for eternity.

"Mama, Mama," Linda cried out, "Mama, Mama, no," she leaned forward and took her into her arms. She held unto the still-warm corpse tightly and began to cry softly, whimpering as waves of pain passed through her body. A doctor put his hand on Linda's shoulder, and in a gentle movement, he closed Linda's mother's eyes. He leaned toward Linda and whispered in her ear, "She's gone now, she's gone." Linda slowly let go and pulled herself back up. She replaced her veil and got up. Veronica and Dawn were right behind her. The three sisters threw themselves into each other's arms and broke into tears. Soon the tears became uncontrollable sobs. Derek just stood by the bed and wiped a silent tear from his cheek. Charles, who was outside the room in the corridor, understood by the sound of the woman's weeping what had just happened.

The passing of her mother was the most difficult time in Linda's life; it was as bitter and as heart-wrenching an occurrence as the accident that had shattered her life. She felt like a part of her had been torn out, brutally and violently. She felt cheated and mad and was inconsolable for days. She had not felt like that when her grandparents had passed away one month apart a few years earlier. She had felt detached from their death for some reason, yet she had loved them both dearly, especially Grandma Flo. At the time she had felt unable to grieve. It was as if she had been so hardened by her own life experience that nothing could touch her. She had sent flowers but had not gone to the funerals. Her mother had been very angry with her about that at the time. But now, faced with the finality of her own mother's death, she felt like she had been savagely attacked by a cruel and invisible enemy. It was as if someone had plunged a knife into her entrails and was prying it about inside her body. She had difficulty moving about, and her bones hurt like they had not hurt for a long time, and the pain that had flooded her heart and soul overtook her body in waves of inextricable pain.

Although each one of her sisters pleaded and insisted that she come and stay with them, Linda checked into the best hotel in town. She spent the days after her mother's death visiting with her sisters and helping them organize the funeral and burial. They reconnected with each other and renewed their sisterly bonds. She got to know their children and husbands and Derek and his wife and kids. It felt good to be close to all of them again, better than Linda had envisioned, and she felt warm and comfortable to be with and about them. Being with them reconnected her with her mother and all that she had been and all she had sacrificed for them.

They all met at Veronica's house after the funeral. The three girls sat at her kitchen table in front of cookies and coffee.

"It's so good to have you here, Linda; we've missed you so much, you know." Dawn placed her hand on Linda's, who kept wiping her tears under her veil with a tissue. It was useless; the tears just kept coming.

"I just wish I had come sooner. Why didn't she tell me she was sick? I would have come, spent some time with her. I could have brought her on a trip—I don't know anything."

"She didn't want you to worry about her, Linda. Plus, she respected your decision to be away. She always defended you on that, always." Dawn's soft voice was soothing. Linda looked toward her.

"Really?"

"Yes, Linda," Veronica added. "She always said it was important for you and that you were doing what you had to do and that eventually you would come back here to us, because we were your family and you loved us all very much." Veronica became choked up with emotion, and she buried her face into a bundle of already soaked tissues. Tears were running freely down her face.

"That sounds so much like Mom. God I miss her," Linda broke down again, sobbing loudly. The crying of her two sisters was too much for Dawn, who broke out into tears too. The three sisters held hands tightly across the table, each trying to console the other and gripping with the most difficult of all pains in the world, the pain of losing one's mother. No matter how young or how old one is, it is the worst pain that exists and reaches far deeper into the very fiber of one's being than one can ever imagine or anticipate. The connection with our entry into the world has been broken and severed forever, creating a deep and vicious open wound that cannot, even by time, be healed. It weighs thus upon our hearts and souls for the remainder of our lives and is the confirmation of our own finiteness.

But pain, even the most unbearable, eventually passes; life must and will continue to claim its preponderance over the living and the ceaseless clamor that is our lives. The intricacies and complexities of day-to-day living eventually retake their hold on everything, imposing a chronology and a pace that one may not choose to deviate or stray from. In the end, it is these imperatives that ultimately bury the dead.

A week after Linda's mother's funeral, Charles came to check in on Linda at 9:30 a.m., as he did every morning. He knocked lightly on the door.

"Come in," Linda said behind the closed door. He let himself in.

"Good morning, miss, how are you today?" He walked up to where Linda was sitting in the living room of the suite. She was dressed in black from head to foot, as she had been since her mother's death.

"I'm fine, Charles, thank you. Please, won't you sit down?" Linda motioned to a sofa in front of her. Charles hesitated; he never sat down with her when he came to check in with her in the morning.

"Please," Linda insisted, pointing toward the sofa. He sat down.

"I have a favor to ask you, Charles." Linda's words hung in the air for a second or two. Charles knew that something unusual was afoot; it was not in Linda's habit to ask him for favors.

"A favor, miss? Well, okay, and what may that favor be?"

"Well, I want you to go back to the city and find a friend of mine and give her this." Linda picked up an envelope from the coffee table beside her; it was a large padded envelope that was filled to capacity. On the envelope in bold letters was written, "Janice" and the address of St. Mary's Mission. Charles looked at the envelope and gently put it down on the sofa beside him. He remained silent, looking intently in her direction.

"Now this friend of mine, she's a very special friend, Charles. That's because Janice, that's her name, my friend, as you can see on the envelope. Well anyway, Janice, she's a homeless person," Linda paused, unsure as to how to continue and obviously uneasy with the situation. Charles looked at her knowingly and cleared his throat.

"May I speak freely, miss?" Linda looked toward him inquisitively.

"Yes, of course, Charles, please do."

"The truth is, miss, I know all about Janice, and I know exactly where to find her. As a matter of fact, I know all your special friends Miss, Janice, Red, and all the other ones. I know that you help these people a lot, and I admire you for that."

"You do?" Linda's was stunned by the revelation.

"Yes, miss, I do. Allow me to explain. You see, I consider it my duty to be aware of everything that concerns you, if I am to do my job properly, that is. To be truthful, though, I found out about what you were doing by accident. I saw you one day in your homeless outfit." Linda was shocked; the thought of Charles seeing her unveiled and in a homeless outfit was not an idea that she found pleasant. "Anyway, I followed you that day, and I've done so ever since—for years, as a matter of fact. I've never told you because I wanted to respect your privacy. You had your reasons for not telling me about this, and it was not for me to ask."

"Charles, you've rendered me speechless. I am amazed that you've known about this for years and have never said a word to me."

"Well, to be honest, miss, this knowledge has been burning me up for some time now. I've been itching to discuss this matter with you, you know, for security reasons and all that. I must tell you that I find you to be a very courageous person, miss, a lot more than most men I know." There was an uncomfortable silence as Linda reflected on what he had just told her.

"Well anyway, miss, I'm glad that this is out in the open now. I was afraid just then that you would invent a story to get me to bring this money to Janice. I would have been terribly embarrassed that you would have had to lie to me, miss, and I do hope this will not affect our relationship in any way." Linda's silence was beginning to worry him. She lifted her head, snapping out of her reverie.

"No, Charles, no, of course not, I'm just surprised, that's all. I don't know what to say."

He rose. "Well, miss, maybe there's nothing else to say. Now if you'll excuse me, I'll go find Janice."

"Yes, Charles, please do, and Charles?"

"Yes."

"Make sure you give that envelope to the nuns. They'll give the money to Janice a little at a time and buy her the things she needs."

"Of course, miss. Is there anything else?"

"No, Charles, nothing else." He turned toward the door. "Charles," she called out after him and he turned around. "Thank you, Charles. Thank you for everything you are and for everything you've done for me." A large smile broke out on his face.

"You're welcome, miss. I'm glad to be of service."

"Drive safely now."

"I will, miss, and I'll see you tomorrow."

"Yes, Charles, see you tomorrow."

Linda spent the rest of the day in her suite immersed in a profound reflection about something that she had been pondering for some time. She had been weighing its pros and its cons ever since her mother's funeral and burial. At the end of the day, her mind was made up. She had decided that her years of wanderings were over and that she would move back to her hometown to live. She wanted to be close to the people she loved and to build a new life for herself.

Charles came to see her in the morning. He had returned late the night before.

"Good morning, miss."

"Good morning, Charles." He walked up to where she was sitting.

"So, tell me, how was Janice?"

"She was fine. A bit on her guard when I approached her, but when I mentioned that I was coming on your behalf, she relaxed a little. We fed the pigeons together, and she asked me a lot of questions about you and where you were. She seemed genuinely concerned, you know, as a friend would. Anyway, I walked with her to the Mission, and I gave the envelope to the nuns, as you instructed. Considering the amount of money there was in that envelope, I guess we can say that things are looking up for Janice." He smiled, pointing his eyes upward. Linda laughed at his allusion to Janice's particular way of walking.

"I guess we can say that, Charles, and thank you for taking care of that for me. I really appreciate it."

"My pleasure, miss."

"Would you please sit down, Charles? I've been thinking a lot lately, and I would like to discuss something with you."

"Of course, miss." He sat down facing her, and she put the cup of coffee she had been holding down on a small table beside her and leaned back in her chair.

"Well, here it is, Charles. I've decided to come back here to live; you know, permanently. I will be looking for a piece of land so I can build a comfortable home for myself. I want to be close to my family, my sisters and brother, and of course, my mother." She choked up, her voice loaded with emotion. The very mention of her mother did that to her. She turned and stared out the window for a moment and then back to Charles. "I'm sorry, Charles. Anyway, I've had enough of the road and the wandering about, and I want to settle down." Charles cleared his throat.

"I think that's an excellent idea, miss. Now tell me, does this plan include that I remain in your service?" The question caught Linda off guard.

"But of course, Charles. My God, what are you saying? I cannot envision life without you, Charles. You have become a dear friend, and I consider you part of my family." Linda was a little panic stricken. The very thought of Charles not being around disturbed her profoundly. "You're part of my life, Charles, and I just don't know what I'd do without you." Her voice had trickled to a whisper, and her breath had become short.

"Thank you, miss, thank you very much. That is the kindest thing anyone has ever said to me. On my part, I can say that I am proud and happy to be in your service and that I have grown quite fond of you over the years. I cannot imagine working for anyone else, and that will hold for as long as you will have me around. I just hope I can continue to live up to the trust and faith that you to put in me."

"I know you will, Charles. I don't have a single doubt about that."

"Well, thank you again then, Miss."

"You're welcome, Charles. You're very welcome."

There was a moment of silence as both of them reflected on what had just been said; it was the first time in all those years they had been together that Linda had so clearly expressed her feelings about him. For some reason she had always kept that to herself, afraid that one day he would get tired of her and go work for somebody else. She had concluded that if she kept her feelings buried deep inside her, it would have made things less painful if he had decided to leave her service.

She cleared her throat.

"Well, now that we've cleared that up, what I wanted to ask you, Charles, was that I hope you won't find this little town too confining or too boring?"

"Of course I will, miss, but we have to go to the city soon for your operation and I'm sure there will be other occasions. Charles was referring to Linda's last of a series of operations she had had over the years and that had straightened out her mouth and that would make her face less horrific to look at. "Bottom line miss, I'm where you are and at your service." Charles spoke with firmness and certainty. Linda was reassured; she had been very concerned about him leaving.

"Thank you, Charles; it makes me very happy to hear you say that." She stretched out her hand, and he took it. They shook hands and smiled to each other. In all those years, it was only the second time they had shaken hands.

"Me too, miss. It makes me very happy too." He let go of her hand and stood up.

"So tell me, miss, when do we start looking for this place to build this home of yours?"

"Tomorrow, Charles. Does tomorrow work for you?"

"Tomorrow works fine for me, miss. Shall we say ten o'clock?"

"Ten o'clock is fine, Charles. I'll be expecting you."

"Okay, miss. So if there's nothing else, I wish you a very pleasant day."

"You too, Charles, have a good day now and once again, thank you."

Linda bought a magnificent piece of land on top of the hill that overlooked the town and the countryside. The view was breathtaking from all angles. On it she had a large, elegant home built. She had it equipped with every modern amenity—indoor and outdoor pools, a Jacuzzi, a sauna, and an entertainment center. She decorated and furnished the place with taste and elegance. Charles acted as her official decorating adviser, accompanying her on every shopping run. The merchants and shopkeepers of the area were very intrigued by this veiled woman dressed in black who walked with a cane and was always accompanied by a tall, impeccably dressed British gentleman. Of course, the fact that they scurried about in a large foreign limo did not help to keep a low profile. Linda and Charles understood that they were a lot for the locals to assimilate and they were careful to be polite and respectful with them at all times.

It took a little over a year for the seventeen-room house to be ready and for Linda and Charles to move in. They both were happy to finally leave the hotel. Charles had his own quarters on the ground floor, and Linda had most of the upstairs. Her room was enormous and was dominated by a king-size bed. There was a very large balcony with an incredible view of the countryside and the mountains at a distance. Linda had hired a live-in housekeeper whose name was Lucille Culiver. Charles had helped Linda find her through one of the agencies that he knew who recommended only top-notch people. Miss Culiver arrived at noon three days after they had moved in. Everything in the house was new and squeaky clean. Linda, dressed in black and veiled, opened the door for her herself.

Lucille Culiver was a tall, thin woman of about forty who stood firm and upright. She was dressed in a conservative fashion and wore no makeup. Linda had seen her picture on her resume and had imagined her shorter and thicker. Even though she dressed down and wore no makeup, Lucille Culiver could not hide the fact that she was a good-looking woman; her features were long and fine, and her thick black hair was tied on her head in a neat bundle and contrasted sharply with the impeccable whiteness of her skin. Her large, round eyes were pale blue, and they had a vivacity and an alertness about them similar to those of a bird of prey.

"Hello, I'm Lucille Culiver." She extended her hand in Linda's direction; her voice was clear and firm in an authoritative kind of way.

"Oh, hi, I'm Linda Staunton." Linda shook her hand. "Please, won't you come in, Miss Culiver?" Linda stepped aside to let her in; she walked in, looking around and up to the ceilings, taking a rapid visual inventory of the place. Lucille Culiver walked in a very upright manner, emanating strength and determination. She turned and looked toward Linda, waiting for instructions as to what was next. Linda pointed toward the living room, where she had planned that they would sit down for their inaugural chat.

The two women sat facing each other. Linda was nervous; they had only talked on the phone twice, and those conversations had been brief and professional. Linda had gone through the whole selection process with Charles. They had passed a number of candidates, and they had finally selected Lucille Culiver. They had checked her references out thoroughly, and Linda had sent her a proposition, conditional to a three-month try out period. When they had spoken on the phone, Linda had described in detail her physical condition and her special needs. Lucille Culiver had not been intimidated by that. She had liked Linda on the phone and had felt good about her. She had wanted to find an unmarried or widowed female employer who lived in the country, and Linda was exactly what she was looking for, so she had accepted the position.

Linda twitched uncomfortably in her sofa.

"Would you like some tea, Miss Culiver?"

"No thank you, Miss Staunton, I'm fine, but please, call me Lucille."

"Very well then, so tell me, Lucille, how was your trip?"

"It was fine, thank you." Lucille Culiver sat upright and was very poised.

"So I see you've just moved in, Miss Staunton." She looked around in a long circular motion.

"Yes, three days ago, actually, a lot of things are not unpacked yet. We're just getting settled in." The other woman's head turned and gave Linda a look. It was only for a split second, but there was fierceness and sharpness in her look. The "we" Linda had used had disturbed her. There had been no "we" in their conversations. Linda caught the vibe.

"I was talking about Charles, Lucille. Charles is my chauffeur. He has been my chauffeur for many years now, and his quarters are on the east side." Linda pointed to her left. "Yours are on the opposite side of the house, adjoining the kitchen. I will introduce you to him when he gets back from town."

"Yes, of course, fine," was her laconic reply, and she seemed to relax a little.

"So you've been in personal services for a long time I understand, Miss Culiver. I mean Lucille."

"Yes, Miss Staunton, I have been in personal services all of my life—as a matter of fact, since I was eighteen, actually. I love it; it's the only job I've ever known and the only one that I wish to know."

"Fine then, so, Lucille, you understand that my physical condition is very different from most people, and as you can see, I am veiled, and I always am in presence of other people. I also dress so as to hide some very ugly scars and the fact that I'm missing a leg and an arm. I think you got the idea over the phone; anyway, it is of the utmost importance to me that my intimacy and privacy be preserved. I am shy about people, and I will be counting on you a lot for that, you know?"

"Of course, Miss Staunton, I fully understand the situation, and I can assure you that I will make this my mission for as long as I am at your service."

The woman chatted for another forty-five minutes, mostly about Lucille's former employers and what her responsibilities would be and how she would organize things. When they were done, Linda stood up and asked, "Maybe I could walk you around the house now and show you where everything is?"

"Yes, that would be fine. Thank you, Miss Staunton."

"Please, call me Linda."

It took only two days for Lucille Culiver to take control of the house. She was a workhorse and a master of organization. Everything, be it deliveries, meals, maintenance, or cleaning, everything came under her watchful ears, eyes, and control. Nothing escaped her, and she made no mistakes. The house became her territory, and she guarded it with an absolute ferocity. Linda and Charles were impressed by her efficiency and aplomb. Charles quickly became very fond of her, and Linda suspected that he had more than professional admiration for the severe yet attractive Miss Culiver, who, like him, was single, well educated, and loved the arts. She spent her evenings reading. It was her passion, especially art history, Charles's favorite subject.

So, life organized itself in a pleasant and comfortable way. After all those years on the road, Linda was happy to be able to settle down and to have a place that she could call home and a place that was close to her mother's spirit. Every week she went to the cemetery to lay flowers on her mother's grave. It was a ritual she never missed, no matter what the weather was, like clockwork, on the same day and at the same time. She was there for about an hour while Charles waited in the car.

Linda kept busy doing little things about the house, but her favorite occupation was taking care of her flower garden. She loved being around her flowers. They filled her with serenity and joy. For her they incarnated life itself, in all its fragility and splendor. Her gardener, Miguel, an immigrant and father of five, came three times a week to tend to her flowers, trees, and lawn. Linda loved to spend time with him. He had a tough, strong feel about him, but in an earthy, grounded kind of way. Miguel loved two things—his family and flowers. He talked to them and cajoled them with his rough, calloused hands, tending to them patiently and giving them what they needed, so that they could explode with the beauty inherent to their genes. He and Linda spent a lot of time outside on the grounds of the mansion, talking about his family or the flowers that they loved. Linda felt good around him; it was as if his sturdy proximity filled her with a sense of security and of belonging, instilling a calmness inside of her, the like of which she had not felt for a long time.

There was only one thing that prevented her from being perfectly happy, and that was her extreme loneliness. It never left her; it was embedded in her being and tore at her insides, constantly haunting her. A lot of nights she would cry herself to sleep; she desperately missed the warmth and the tenderness of another human being, the magic of being close to someone, to touch, to kiss, and to caress, to hold and to belong to. It was her condemnation and her cross to bear and would be, she believed, until the day she died. "It's so bloody unfair," she kept repeating to herself, "so bloody unfair, to have so much love to give and no one to give it to." At night she would often stand alone on her balcony imploring the heavens. "You God, or whoever or whatever is out there, I know my body is deformed and repulsive, but my soul is more beautiful now than my body has ever been. Why do I have no one to share this with, why?" Of course, there were never any answers that came from the heavens, and the only living things beside her family that Linda could shower her love upon were her three cats and two dogs. She called them her "little rays of sunshine" and spent endless hours petting them and caring for them. There was nothing however, that could assuage the profound forlornness that inhabited her heart.

Although Linda did not travel the country anymore, she kept in touch with all of her former haunts. She sent donations every year to every shelter or mission she had been to. It was her way of staying in contact with all the friends she had made among the homeless and the dispossessed. Although she was not in their midst, she thought of them often—the other people, the ones who had accepted her as she was and had not judged her on her appearance. They were the only people to whom she had revealed herself completely, and she had been one of them. She missed them dearly; her friends and acquaintances, and she missed spending times with them. It was a strong emotion when it came to her, and it pulled her in the direction of hitting the road again, but then something beautifully domestic would happen, and she would forget her broodings and return to her tranquil daily preoccupations.

One morning, Linda was in her room lounging in bed with her cats when Lucille knocked. Linda veiled herself and called out, "Come in." Lucille stepped into the room.

"I'm sorry to disturb you, miss, but there's a man at the door who wants to speak to you." She seemed ill at ease, unsure of herself, and that was definitely not in her character.

"Well, who is he, Lucille?"

Hesitantly, she replied, "He says he's your father." Lucille had a troubled look on her face, and her pale skin seemed paler than usual.

Linda sat motionless and speechless for what seemed like a long time, and then in a very calm voice she said, "Oh really, wow! Well okay, then, Lucille, bring him in the living room. I'll be down shortly." Linda's tone was firm and decisive, even though the thought of meeting her father after all those years scared her half to death.

"Fine," the firmness of her persona had returned in Lucille's voice, and she left the room. Although Linda had wanted to sound reassuring in front of Lucille, the truth was quite the contrary, and she began to shake like a leaf and felt nauseous. She had a sudden urge to vomit and rushed to the bathroom. When she got back from the bathroom, she slowly began to get dressed, still feeling a bit shaken.

"My father, my father," she kept repeating in her head. "Can you believe that? Can you believe the audacity he has, of showing up here?" Linda was stunned and incredulous. She kept shaking her head in disbelief, and rage was slowly building up inside of her. She had not seen her father since she was nine years old, and no matter how hard she tried, she couldn't visualize him. The truth was that she just couldn't remember him. She remembered how she had hated and cursed him when she was young, though, for all the pain and suffering that he had put them through. She remembered that well. It was something that she would never forget.

When she was ready, she took a deep breath and slowly made her way downstairs toward the living room. Lucille had set it up as she always did when Linda had to meet people. The idea was that the visitors saw as little of her as was necessary. All the shades were drawn, and there were lamps at the three extremities of the room. Lucille would always sit the visitor on a large couch partially lit by one of the nearby lamps, as she had just done; a man was sitting on the sofa. Linda came in from the opposite end of the living room and made her way to a large armchair off to one side, the part of the room that had the least light. She was dressed all in black and veiled; quietly, she put her cane to her side and sat down, comfortable and calm in the semi-darkness. She felt in control now as she looked intensely toward the broad-shouldered man of sixty or so who sat on the sofa across from her. He was partially bald, overweight, and unshaven; his clothes were disheveled and dirty. He was twisting and turning his hands nervously, and sweat was apparent on his forehead. He squinted in Linda's direction when she entered and shuffled his feet about back and forth. Linda did not move, although her heart was beating fast. She felt secure behind her veil; she waited in silence to see what would happen.

He smiled sheepishly in her direction, bobbing his head from left to right. Roy Staunton was intimidated by the luxurious surroundings and the semi-darkness; he had never been in a house like this before. He decided to break the awkward silence.

"Hi, Linda, it's good to see you. I guess you don't remember me much, eh?"

"How could I forget you? You abandoned us when I was nine, remember?" Linda's voice was harsh and filled with bitterness. The sight of him was making her blood boil; she was seething inside and as close as she had ever come in her life to actually feeling hatred for someone.

He had come prepared for her anger and was ready to face it.

"Look, Linda, I know you probably don't like me and all, but I am your father. I mean, that does mean something, you know."

"Oh yeah, says who? And you know what else? As far as I'm concerned, you're dead and buried, so don't give me this father bullshit, okay? I'm not buying today." Linda was surprised at the harshness of her own words.

"Look, Linda, will you just bear with me and hear me out please?" He had raised his voice a bit. Linda had upset him. "I mean, just because you have money doesn't mean you can be miss high and mighty with me, you know." He looked about the room to emphasize his point. Linda did not reply. She was too afraid of her own rage, and he took her silence as his cue to continue speaking.

"I know you guys had it rough back then, but I've had some rough times too. I mean, I've had to fend for myself out there. I know what it's like. I didn't make out too good neither, you know, doing odd jobs, making just enough money to be able to eat and to have a place to sleep. Being treated like a bum and being cheated by everyone." He was practically whining now, playing the victim, as he had done all his life. "Plus, I've been sick lately, real bad, you know, Linda. I've got diabetes and hypertension too, no insurance and no pension, so things are really tough. I mean, it's been bad before, but never like this. You understand, eh, Linda? You hear what I'm saying, right? I mean, most days I don't even have anything to eat, or money to buy my medicine. It's bloody awful to hit bottom at my age, Linda, bloody awful." He paused and looked in her direction, hoping that he was succeeding in appealing to her compassion and sympathy.

It suddenly dawned on Linda why he was there; it was not to beg for her forgiveness as she had assumed, or to be reunited with her and her siblings. He wanted money; he had come to beg for money. She was stunned by his shamelessness and gall, and she felt even angrier. He continued, oblivious to the mounting fury building up inside of her.

"So anyway, when I heard from a buddy of mine that you'd come back here, I decided to come to see you. I mean, we're family, right? So I figured I have to go see her and tell her how bad I'm doing. I'm sure she'll understand. I mean, I can't even work no more, Linda. What's a man to do if he can't work? He can't take care of himself, and he's got no dignity left, no more self-esteem, nothing. I mean, I know what I did back then, running away from your mom and you guys, I know that was wrong, dammed wrong. You think I don't know that? Of course I do. And you know what? I've regretted that every day of my life. Linda, not a day has gone by that I didn't think about you, your mother, and brother and sisters, not one, I swear. God be my witness." He pointed toward the ceiling.

"I'd have sent money, Linda; I swear I would have, if I could have. I just never got a good day going, even for myself. I mean, I barely survived all those years. I only wished I could have helped you. It broke my heart, all of that, Linda, I swear it did, and many a time I just wanted to finish it all and to end my miserable existence." His voice had become shaky, as if his emotions were getting the better of him. Roy Staunton was a lifetime loser and a manipulator extraordinaire, and today, sensing a big payday, he was going for the jugular.

"I loved you guys. I loved you more than anything in the world. I swear I did, but I fell on hard times back then. I lost my job, and your mother just kept screaming at me to get it together and I lost it. I mean, I just lost it. I'm sorry, Linda, I'm really sorry." He bent his head forward, looking to the floor. Linda was seething, and the thought that he should blame her mother for anything sent her over the top.

"How dare you talk about her, you bastard? You're the one who put her in her grave before her time, and you didn't even have the decency to come to her funeral. Don't you ever say anything bad about her again, not in this house and not in my presence, ever, do you hear me?" Linda had raised her voice; she could not help herself. His whining, pathetic presence was an aggression on every single cell of her body. He was taken aback by her tone, and so he decided to change approach. He spoke softly, pleading with her.

"Okay, Linda, I hear you okay, but look, I loved your mother too, you know. I know you probably don't believe that right now, but she was the woman of my dreams. She was everything to me. I loved her more than anything in the world. But I blacked out. Okay, I panicked, and I bolted, and then later I was too ashamed to come back even though I thought about doing it often. I know I shouldn't have left like that. I know that now, but I did, and I'm very sorry for all the pain and suffering I put you guys through and I will be till the day I die." He lowered his head and put his face into his hands for a moment, as if he were crying. "Do you think you'll ever be able to forgive me, Linda?" He whimpered, "Do you?" He slowly raised his head, and Linda saw that his eyes were dry, and she remained silent.

"You know I only found out a few years ago about your accident. I cried when I heard about that. I mean, you're still my little girl, Linda, you know. God I wish I could have done something for you. Then recently I heard of your mother's death. It broke my heart, Linda, I swear it did. God I loved that woman. I would have come to the funeral, but I was too ashamed, ashamed of myself and of having to face all of you." He put his face in his hands again and bowed his head again, shaking his shoulders a bit as if in tears. With his head still down, he asked her again.

"Do you think you can forgive me, Linda? Do you think that you can find it in your heart to forgive me and help me in my old age?" He raised his head, staring across the semi-dark room, trying to see her more clearly, but he could only make out her black, veiled silhouette, immobile and stoic.

"Is that why you came here, Roy?" Linda used his first name to affirm her command of the situation. "To ask for my forgiveness and for some money? To say you're sorry for what happened, or is it just the money, Roy? What will it be?

"Well, it's all of that." He was irritated by her tone. "I'm getting old, Linda, and I want to receive your forgiveness before it's too late. It's important to me, Linda. I pray now, you know. God has entered my life, and I go to church every week. I pray for you and for your brother and sisters. I think God would want you to forgive me and to help me, Linda, don't you think so?"

"I haven't spoken to him recently, Roy, so I don't know what he wants or doesn't want me to do." Linda's sarcasm was acerbic; she was disgusted by the poor excuse of a man who sat in front of her. As far as she was concerned, her father was a loser and a drunk. He always had been and always would be.

"There you go you're angry. I knew you'd be angry at me. I shouldn't have come; that's why I hesitated for so long.

Don't you see? I'm just a broken, sick old man asking for your forgiveness. Is that too much to ask?" He had raised his voice; he was angry and frustrated at how little effect his pleas were having on his daughter.

Hearing him raise his voice that way reminded Linda of when he used to beat his mother when he came home drunk, she remembered that tone of voice well, and she became incensed. She had had enough of Roy Staunton.

"I'll tell you what I see, Roy, you son of a bitch. I see the bastard that abandoned my mother, my brother, my sisters, and me when the oldest of us was nine years old. That's what I see, Roy; do you know the hardships we went through? Do you have any idea of the misery and pain that you inflicted on us? Do you? Do you know how many nights we went to bed hungry?" Linda was shouting now. Never in her life had she been this angry with another human being. Her father tried to respond, but she cut him off brutally.

"Shut up," she screamed. "I'm talking now. I've heard enough of your crap, you son of a bitch. Do you know what it's like to have no clothes to go to school with, to have no presents at Christmas, to be the poorest people in this town? Do you? Do you know how hard mom had to work to feed us and provide a roof over our heads? Do you know, Roy? Do you?" The power and rage of Linda's voice reduced him to silence. He knew that tone; he could feel the violence and the danger in her voice. Linda's screaming brought Lucille into the room; she stood upright in the middle of the room between Linda and her father.

"Is everything okay, miss?" She looked from one to the other, eying Linda's father with a severity that said, "You had better not move." Using her cane, Linda got to her feet.

"No, Lucille, everything is not okay. I want you to escort this scumbag out of my house, this whining, cheating bastard, get him out of here, now." Linda was screaming and pointing her cane in his direction; tears were running down her cheeks under her veil, and she was trembling from head to foot.

Lucille was stunned by Linda's vocabulary and screaming, but she did as she was told. She walked over to Linda's father and stood firmly in front of him, hands on her waist.

"Okay, you heard her. Follow me now, please." She looked him straight in the eyes with a look that said, "You had better obey me, or all hell will break loose." Roy Staunton got up; he looked over Lucille's shoulder toward Linda pleadingly.

"Sir, please, let's go now." Lucille's voice was sharp and incisive; she took a step forward and grabbed him firmly by the arm.

He pulled his arm from her grip roughly and began to walk toward the door with Lucille in tow, his shoulders drooping, crushed by his failure to gain his daughter's sympathy or help. As he walked out the door, Linda shouted, "Don't ever come back here again, Roy Staunton, ever, do you hear me? You're dead. You're dead and buried." Roy Staunton did not respond. He just walked away and never looked back, as he had done so many years before.

Linda sat back down in her chair, shaking from head to foot. Tears were still rolling down her face. Her shoulders began to shake, and she began to sob uncontrollably. She was in shock; her whole being in turmoil, she was surprised by the vehemence and force of her own anger.

Lucille came back from the front door and walked over to where Linda was sitting. She leaned down and put a hand on Linda's shaking shoulder and said softly, "May I get you something, miss?" Lucille's voice was filled with warmth and genuine sympathy. Linda took a deep breath.

"Yes, Lucille, bring me a cognac, please. I think I really need one right now," she managed to say between the sobs.

When Lucille returned with the cognac, Linda gulped it down in one shot. Lucille just stood there, not sure as to what to do next. Linda looked up in her direction and took her hand, squeezing it hard.

"I'm okay, Lucille. I'm sorry about the shouting; I was just beyond myself with rage. I'm sorry about all that, I mean …" Lucille patted her hand gently,

"It's okay, miss, I understand. You do not have to explain."

"Thank you, Lucille. I'll just sit here a while and try to calm down. You go ahead and do what you have to do. I'll be fine, really."

"Okay, if you need anything, just call me."

"I will thank you." Linda let go of her hand, and Lucille left, leaving her alone with her thoughts.

Linda sat for a long time in her chair in the semi-darkness, her anger unabated. She cried until she had no more tears left to shed, her heart broken by her father for the second time in her life. Her years of traveling had given her the strength and experience to see her father for what he was, but she had hated every second of his visit. It had opened up a wound she had forgotten she had, but it was real and deep and difficult. It had been one of the most upsetting moments of her life, and she kept repeating to herself the same thing over and over again: "You bastard, Roy Staunton, you goddamn bastard. I hate you. I hate your bloody guts."

The incident of her father's return was followed by another similar one a few months later. One Sunday Linda had all her family over for lunch, as she did most Sundays. The house was filled with children, pets, and family. It was the best time of any week for Linda, to be with the people she loved and to share some quality time with them and to do what families do when they are reunited. Linda had never told her brother or sisters about their father's visit to her a few months before. She had decided for all of them that he was part of the past. That's how things had been, and that's how things would stay. No one ever talked about him anyway, and as far as all were concerned, it was as if he were dead already.

"So Linda, did you hear?" Linda and Veronica were sitting at the table after the meal, and everyone else was outside or about the house somewhere.

"Hear what?"

"You remember Richard Benson, right?"

The name Richard Benson jolted Linda, even after all those years, how could she forget him—Richard, her Richard. An old familiar ache began to build up in her chest.

"Of course I remember Richard. We were together for a while, you know."

"Yeah, I know. Well anyway, I heard that he's back in town."

"Oh really," Linda feigned disinterest.

"I heard from someone who knows his mother. He's staying at her place apparently."

"Oh really? What about his family? I mean, he surely has a family. Where are they?"

"There is no family, only him. He never married, it seems—no wife, no kids. My friend told me that he went through some very tough times; he had some kind of football accident or something when he was young and …" Just then, Veronica's oldest daughter Mia came running in to fetch her mother.

"Mommy, Mommy, come outside, Daddy wants you to come." She took her mother's hand, trying to get her to stand up.

"Okay, okay, I'm coming. I'm sorry, Linda." She got up and followed her daughter outside.

Linda was flustered; she was surprised at how disturbed and moved she was by the simple mention of Richard's name. She hadn't thought of him in years and had practically forgotten him. "What if I meet him by chance?" she wondered. "What if he wants to see me? What will I do? Does he know how bad my condition is?" All these questions kept turning in her mind for the rest of the afternoon and for a long time after her family had left.

She had forgotten her turmoil of the previous Sunday when one week later Lucille told her that there was a phone call for her.

"Who is it Lucille?"

"Someone called Richard; he says he's an old friend of yours."

Linda was stunned. What she had feared was happening. She picked up the phone and put it to her ear, but no sound came out of her mouth. She was unable to speak.

"Linda, Linda, are you there?" Richard had heard the sound of the phone being picked up.

"Yes," her voice was barely audible.

"Linda, it's me, Richard."

"Hi," she answered hesitantly.

"It's so nice to hear your voice, Linda. How are you?"

"I'm fine, thank you, and you?" Linda was in a state of shock.

"Well, that's a long story, Linda. I've had a bit of a rough patch, but I'm okay now. I just moved back here, you know?"

"Yes, I heard, my sister told me." Linda was petrified; she could not bring herself to speak, except in forced monosyllabic phrases.

"Well look, Linda, is there any way we could have coffee or something? You know, for old time's sake. I'd love to see you again." The word "see" pierced Linda's heart.

"Well uh, yes, I …" He quickly picked up on her hesitation.

"Look, Linda, I heard about your accident and all that's happened to you, okay? I know what shape you're in. People have told me, so don't worry; its okay. I understand. I mean, you're still Linda, aren't you? The Linda I knew, you're the same person, right? Now that hasn't changed, has it?" Linda relaxed a little. His words helped to slightly assuage her anguish.

"Yes, Richard, I'm still Linda, that hasn't changed." Linda smiled, and a warm, pleasant feeling invaded her body. For a split second she felt like she had felt when they had been together. It seemed like such a long time ago to her now.

"I'll tell you what, Linda; we'll only meet if and when you feel like it and on your own terms, okay? Whenever you feel you're ready, let me know and I'll be there. Promise me you'll think about it, please?"

"Okay, Richard, I will, I promise." Linda regretted having said that the second she had said it. The truth was that she was terrified at the thought of him ever seeing her again.

"Good, do you have a pen nearby? I'll give you my phone number, and that way you can call me, you know when you're ready."

"Yes, of course, just give me a second." Linda's hand trembled as she jotted down his number.

"Thank you for calling, Richard. I'll call you soon, okay?" She pronounced the words, but in her mind she had no intention of ever calling him back, and she desperately wanted the phone conversation to be over.

"Promise me you will?" he insisted gently before hanging up.

"Yes, I promise," Linda whispered the last words and then hung up. Her head was spinning; she turned around and headed toward the living room. She sat down and did not move for a long time. She was in a daze and unable to think straight. "Richard Benson!" She kept repeating in her head, "Richard Benson! What am I going to do about that?"

The idea of seeing him again tortured her for days; she just could not get him out of her head, and it made her agitated and restless. How would he react to her physical state, she wondered? Was he strong enough? Did he have what it takes to deal with her condition? The fact that he had sounded so nice on the phone was a big plus; he had nearly made her feel comfortable. But what would happen when he saw her in person? After turning this around in her head for a few days, Linda made a decision. She would have him over, and if it was too much for him, well then, so be it. He would be off and that would be the end of that. Linda knew that she could run into him when she was in town doing errands with Charles, and that would have been very embarrassing, especially if she had not called him back. So she decided that it was better to confront him on her territory and to get it over with. She called him back and invited him for coffee the next afternoon at three.

By the time he arrived, Linda had been sitting in the semi-darkness of the living room for over twenty minutes. She was nervous but determined to see this through. Lucille let Richard in; Linda looked him over as Lucille indicated to him where he should sit. He still had a good, solid body, but his hair was thinning and that made him look a little older than his age. He also had a very bad limp when he walked, and when he sat down it was obvious that he could not bend his leg much. It stuck out at an angle in front of him.

IAN TREMBLAY

"Hi, Richard," Linda said from behind her veil.

He looked over in her direction, squinting, trying to adjust to the light of the room.

"Oh hi, Linda, I didn't realize you were sitting there." He was obviously ill at ease; the situation was probably not what he had imagined. Linda helped him along.

"So, what's with the limp, Richard?"

"Well, that's a long story, Linda. Want to hear it?"

"Yes I would, Richard; I'd like that very much"

"Okay, then. Well, in my last year at college, I had a very bad football accident. I broke my leg in four places, smashed it good, and that was the end of my football career. Bang, just like that, in two seconds, all was finished and the life I had dreamed about was over."

"I'm sorry to hear that, Richard, I didn't know."

"Hey, it's okay, don't worry about it. I've gotten over that now. It hit me hard at the time, though, Linda. I mean here I was the school hero. I was pampered and idolized. Everything was given to me, and whatever I wanted, I had. There were agents all over me to represent me and scouts from a lot of teams who came to see me play. I was floating on a river of endless praise and worship, me being the object of that worship and praise, of course. It never dawned on me that it was all fragile and nonrenewable. I didn't know what it was like to be vulnerable and to feel pain—real pain, that is. I think if anybody can understand what I mean by that, it's certainly you." Linda nodded her head in approval. "Anyway, to make a long story short, there I was on top of the world, for about five minutes, that is, if you consider the time frame of our lives. Then, when this happened," he pointed to his stiff leg, "that was it, no more hero, no more nothing, game over. I had seven operations on my leg; I went into a deep depression when the doctors told me I would never play football again. I just couldn't believe it was all over. My grades, which were already so-so, as you know, took a permanent direction south. I became addicted to painkillers and pills of all kinds and anything else I could get my hands on. Well, that, combined with a major drinking problem I'd developed, made me a complete basket case. I was totally wiped out. No more friends, no more money, no more glory, no more nothing. I lost everything, and mostly, though, I lost myself, and I ended up on the street and became a homeless person, a vagrant and a bum. Can you believe that? Me, Richard Benson, my mother would have died had she known the truth about what and how I was living. I lived for seven years that way, Linda, out there." He pointed behind himself. "They were years of darkness, Linda, complete darkness. I was a lost soul, drowning in my misery and in alcohol. I swear, most of it I don't even remember. That's how out of it I was."

Linda couldn't help but imagining the improbable situation that could have happened. She could have met up with him in her homeless outfit and unveiled, during one of her numerous visits of skid rows or shelters, as had been her habit for so many years, albeit for very different reasons. "Wow, that would certainly have been a shock," she thought, and the thought sent a shiver down her spine. Richard continued his story.

"So anyway, one day I hit rock bottom, and this ex-alcoholic, ex-drug addict—Anthony, that was his name—Anthony, well he saved my life. The only reason I'm not dead is because of him. He helped me sober up, get my head back together, and become a human being again. He brought me back to life, and he showed me how to feel good about myself again. I owe him everything that guy, Linda, everything. If it weren't for him, I'd be dead and buried for sure." He bowed his head, moving his intertwined hands nervously in front of him, his eyes staring into space as he reflected on his past. Linda cleared her throat, breaking the awkward silence.

"Wow, that's nearly as bad as my own story, Richard." His honesty and vulnerability touched her. She felt much better in his presence than she would have thought, a bit like she had felt with her friends Red and Janice and all the other street people she had befriended in her years of wanderings.

"Yeah, I know you had it bad, Linda, real bad. People around here told me. I'm really sorry about that. I really feel for you, and my heart reaches out to you. But hey, you're alive, right? And you're still Linda. That's all that matters really, you know."

"Yes, I am, Richard. I'm still Linda. I'm a different person, you know, physically, but inside, it's still me." He was smiling at her, and if he could have seen her face behind her veil, he would have seen that she was smiling too.

"There is something else I want to tell you, Linda. It's important to me. It's about Diane Sorenson." Linda interrupted him.

"You don't have to, Richard, I know, someone told me about her a few years ago, an ex-friend of hers. I know that she purposely and wickedly tore us apart; I know the whole story, Richard, and I really pity her. She must have been a very unhappy person to do what she did." There was no rage or anger in Linda's voice; she had come to terms with that chapter of her life a long time ago.

"I see. Well, I only found out after she dumped me, you know, and that was not too long after I broke my leg. I was lying in a hospital bed, and I'd just found out that I'd never play football again. Perfect timing eh? Anyway, she told me the whole story herself. She was proud of that and laughed in my face. I was beyond stunned; I just couldn't believe that someone could be mean like that. Well anyway, she went off and married some corporate big-shot guy, I heard, didn't even finish school; she's probably very busy screwing up his life right now, eh?"

"Yes, Richard, I'm sure she's still out there hurting someone. But don't worry; life will catch up with her. Life always does sooner or later, you know."

"Yeah, you're right about that. Well, whatever. I just wanted to set the record straight by you."

"The record is set straight, Richard. It's all ancient history now."

Just then Lucille entered the room with a tray of coffee and cookies. She served them in silence; she felt that this was a time to be silent and respectful. It was something in the air, something that she sensed was there and that was about the room.

"Thank you, Lucille. Oh, Lucille, this is a very dear and very old friend of mine, Richard Benson. We went to high school together." Lucille bowed her head slightly toward Richard and smiled at him, not her stiff, professional smile, but a more generous and sincere one.

"Pleased to meet you, sir," Richard tried to get up to shake her hand, but he failed in his attempt to do so because of his leg, and he fell back in his chair. Sheepishly, he extended his hand to Lucille, who took it, and they shook hands.

"Sorry about that." He pointed to his leg, slightly embarrassed.

"It's okay, sir, I understand."

"Well anyway, I'm glad to meet you too, Lucille. Thank you for the coffee and the cookies." He smiled, and his smile was generous and innocent, and Lucille smiled back. It was at that instant that Linda realized that deep down; Richard was still the pure innocent boy she had known in her youth. He was still the same good, kind-hearted person she had known and that she had loved and cherished.

"You're welcome, sir. Will that be all, miss?" Lucille asked, turning toward Linda.

"Yes, thank you, Lucille." Just as she turned to go, Linda asked, "Oh, just one more thing, Lucille. Are you and Charles still going to that concert tonight?" Linda asked with a touch of mischief in her voice. Lucille looked at Linda with her stoic, professional look.

"Yes, miss, of course. You know how fond he is of classical music, and I'm glad to accompany him, if that's still okay with you, of course?" She was slightly defensive.

"Of course its okay Lucille, don't be silly. Just make me a tuna salad and leave it in the fridge, will you please? I'll have a light dinner and retire early."

"Yes, of course, miss, but you're sure it's okay that I go?"

"Of course I'm sure. You just go and enjoy yourself and don't worry about me. I'll be fine."

Lucille smiled stiffly and left the room. Linda chuckled to herself; she was now sure that Charles and Lucille were very fond of each other and that they had a little thing going on. Charles had not said it directly to her, but she had sensed it in her conversations with him. When he mentioned Lucille his voice would change, and he had trouble hiding his affection for her. Linda was happy about that. She loved them both dearly and wished only the best for them.

"Sorry about that, Richard, just a little domestic business."

"No problem, Linda. Hey, by the way, this is a really beautiful home you have here." Richard looked in all directions, nodding his head approvingly.

"Thank you. I like it very much here; it has a nice feel to it. Maybe I can show you around later?"

"I'd love that, Linda." He smiled in her direction; he had had some apprehensions about coming, but now he was glad that he had done so, and he felt good about being close to Linda again.

They chatted for over four hours, and time flew by. The conversation flowed naturally between them, and they both enjoyed being in each other's company. Richard even got Linda to laugh a few times when he told her about some of his funnier skid row adventures. He voluntarily omitted the murkier and more sinister situations that he had so often been into. Of course, what he did not know is that Linda knew exactly what he was talking about. She had decided not to share with him right away her own experience of that world. Linda told him all about her college years and how she had loved working with animals, even if it had only been for a short time. Then, she told him about her accident, sharing with him all the details of her physical pain and psychological distress. She told him things that she had never told anyone else, besides her mother, that is. She felt she could tell him everything and that it would be all right. It felt good to share her more intimate thoughts with someone again, someone that she knew and that she felt she could trust. She told him about her difficult rehabilitation and the cruelty of the world for someone disfigured and handicapped like her and about the loneliness and the solitude. She talked about her family and her mother's death, leaving out her father's unexpected return a month before and her violent reaction to that.

Richard listened intently, in silence and respect, asking questions here and there, and when he spoke, it was in a soft, soothing tone, and his voice was like music to Linda's ears. He shared with her the pathetic story of what his life had been since they had been separated, of his descent into hell and his many brushes with death. He told her some of the worst things he had done or that had happened to him, at least the ones he could remember. He was not proud of where he had been and what he had done, but in order to heal, he explained to her that it was important that he share with other human beings the depths to which he had fallen. He told her that he had hit his lowest point when his father died. His mother had been unable to reach him, and he had never made it to the funeral or the burial. He had only found out a year later, and it had broken his mother's heart. He was very ashamed of that, and he said he would never forgive himself. He explained to Linda that he lived with his mother now and that he was trying to make good by her for all the years that he had forgotten and neglected her. He worked at the local library and had no one in his life; as a matter of fact, he had never married. Both he and Linda were so absorbed in telling their respective stories that neither of them saw the time pass. In a way, it felt like they had never been apart.

When they had finally talked themselves out, there was an awkward silence for a second or two. Richard got up and slowly hobbled across the half-lit room toward Linda. Her heart lurched and began to beat fast when she saw him coming in her direction. With great difficulty because of his stiff leg, Richard got down on one knee in front of her. He took her scarred hand into his and stroked it gently and kissed it. Her hand trembled, and she felt that he could see her through the veil when he looked at her. She was speechless and did not know what to do or say. It had been years since a man had taken her hand that way, and she had forgotten what it felt like.

"Linda, I just want to tell you that for me, you're the only woman who has ever meant anything in my life. I don't care what you look like; it's of no importance to me. I loved you back then, more than myself and more than life itself, as I love you now, Linda, and I always will. I came here to be sure of that, and now I am sure. I've never stopped loving you, Linda, never, even in the darkest moments of my existence; my heart always has and always will belong to you and to you alone. Being here today and talking to you—well, I'm just overwhelmed by the feelings that are exploding inside of me. I know I hurt you in the past, Linda. I hurt you bad," tears began to roll down his face, "I beg you to forgive me and to open your heart to me again. Please, Linda, I swear I'll make it up to you. I swear on everything that I hold sacred and holy. I want to be with you, Linda, for the rest of my life. There is no doubt in my heart; I would be the happiest person in the world if you accepted." Overcome by his emotions, Richard bowed his tear-drenched face and kissed her hand again, holding it with both of his. His large shoulders began to shake, and he let out a few muffled sobs.

Linda was overtaken by Richard's sudden declaration and surge of emotions. Tears rolled down her face too, she squeezed Richard's hand and whispered, "Oh Richard, Richard." She gasped for air and raised his hands to her lips beneath her veil, kissing them tenderly and drenching them with her tears.

"I love you too, Richard. I've always loved you, and I'll always love only you."

Richard threw himself into her lap, wrapping his arms around her waist, holding her tightly and sobbing like a baby. Linda gently stroked his hair and caressed his face.

"Oh, Linda, Linda, I'm so sorry, so sorry. God I love you." He slowly raised his head and looked at her; his eyes were filled with tears and with the unconditional love he felt for her.

She bent her head toward him and lifted her veil and kissed his face and tears and gently passed her lips on his.

"Promise me we'll be together for the rest of our lives, Linda, promise me," he managed to say through his sobs.

"I promise, Richard, I promise."

THE END

ABOUT THE AUTHOR

Ian Tremblay is an indie author who works in the entertainment business and is an avid world traveller and fishing aficionado. He studied English Literature and has published three other books, *Tales of Inhumanity and Retribution, Tales of Duplicity and Discontent* and *The Illegal and the Refugee-An American Love Story.*

Some of the individual stories of his first two books are in the process of being made available in paperback and on all digital platforms. The first two stories, *Aisha-A Tale of Retribution and The Death and Life of Gustav Henn* have been published in 2015.

Rich Homeless Broken But Beautiful is the third and is the story of Linda Staunton, a strikingly beautiful young woman who experiences a life changing traumatic event and more pain and heartache before she is twenty-five than most people do in a lifetime. She eventually learns to face her challenges and then slowly discovers her inner strength and the curative powers of the heart. If you wish to find out more about the author go to his website **www.iantremblay.com**

www.ingramcontent.com/pod-product-compliance
Lightning Source LLC
Chambersburg PA
CBHW071506170626
46811CB00007B/2751